CATCH AND
SADDLE

Also by L. P. Holmes
in Large Print:

Desert Rails
Payoff at Pawnee
Shadow of the Rim
Somewhere They Die
Apache Desert
Bloody Saddles
The Savage Hours
Rustler's Moon
The Distant Vengeance
Flame of Sunset
The Plunderers
High Starlight
Night Marshal

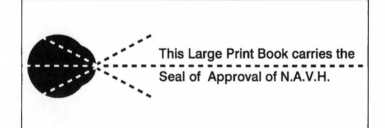

This Large Print Book carries the
Seal of Approval of N.A.V.H.

CATCH AND SADDLE

L. P. HOLMES

Thorndike Press • Waterville, Maine

Published in 2005 by arrangement with Golden West Literary Agency.

Thorndike Press® Large Print Western.

The tree indicium is a trademark of Thorndike Press.

The text of this Large Print edition is unabridged.
Other aspects of the book may vary from the original edition.

Set in 16 pt. Plantin by Al Chase.

Printed in the United States on permanent paper.

Library of Congress Cataloging-in-Publication Data

Holmes, L. P. (Llewellyn Perry), 1895–
    Catch and saddle / by L.P. Holmes.
        p. cm. — (Thorndike Press large print Westerns)
    ISBN 0-7862-7588-X (lg. print : hc : alk. paper)
    1. Ranchers — Fiction.   2. Large type books.   I. Title.
    II. Thorndike Press large print Western series.
    PS3515.O4448C38 2005
    813′.52—dc22   2005002902

CATCH AND SADDLE

As the Founder/CEO of NAVH, the only national health agency solely devoted to those who, although not totally blind, have an eye disease which could lead to serious visual impairment, I am pleased to recognize Thorndike Press* as one of the leading publishers in the large print field.

Founded in 1954 in San Francisco to prepare large print textbooks for partially seeing children, NAVH became the pioneer and standard setting agency in the preparation of large type.

Today, those publishers who meet our standards carry the prestigious "Seal of Approval" indicating high quality large print. We are delighted that Thorndike Press is one of the publishers whose titles meet these standards. We are also pleased to recognize the significant contribution Thorndike Press is making in this important and growing field.

Lorraine H. Marchi, L.H.D.
Founder/CEO
NAVH

* Thorndike Press encompasses the following imprints: Thorndike, Wheeler, Walker and Large Print Press.

ONE

The storm caught up with him as he reached the first fringe of the timber.

A score of times throughout this day's long ride across the open plain he had twisted in his saddle to measure the full portent of the elemental tumult mounding behind him. A solid front of gray-black clouds, wind-whipped, scudding, moiling. Like something alive, remorselessly intent on pursuit. So he kept the roan steadily at it, striking for the shelter of the timbered hills which beckoned from the north.

Now, even though he had gained that shelter, he knew he was in for it. With the storm's arrival, all was tearing wind and a sheeting downpour, flailing the tree tops. For a short time only did this lofty canopy protect. Then, gorged with rain, the timber spilled its full wetness down, and Clay Hanford and his roan mount moved through a drenching, darkening world.

There was a trail of sorts which the roan found and fell into. Hanford did not argue the point. This was new country to him, and he had no idea what lay immediately ahead. But all trails led somewhere, and there was no better answer at the moment than to gamble on this one.

The sky's piled up blackness held more than wind and rain. Lightning lanced a spectral light across the world, fractional in its visual evidence, savage in its intensity. After which, thunder smashed massively.

The roan came to a near halt, snorting, swinging an uneasy head.

"Sure, Blue — sure!" Hanford murmured. "That stuff scares hell out of me, too. But we got to go along."

So they went along, while lightning scarred the heavens again and again and thunder boomed an endless cannonade through the deepening gloom. The smell of ozone, raw and biting, charged the air.

With the first impact of the storm met and absorbed, Clay Hanford stoically locked his inner self away from the punishment of the elements. Chill wetness engulfed him completely, and the prospect of a night in the open of this wildly shouting world was a dismal one. Yet there was nothing left to do but endure.

Time and distance fell away. The lightning and the thunder moved on to sear and bludgeon the higher reaches of these hills, leaving behind a burly, crowding wind, and a rain which fell without letup.

Abruptly the trail leveled and the timber thinned and then the roan was splashing belly-deep in the hurrying waters of a storm-swollen creek. Clumps of willow, windlashed and writhing, lined the creek, and in a little meadow beyond these, the low bulk of a cabin crouched in the streaming, half-drowned dusk.

Lunging, the roan drove across the short stretch of heavy current, broke through the willows on the far bank and lined straight for the cabin at a reaching trot.

The cabin was of logs, small but sturdy, with a lean-to stable against its back wall. There was no sign of anyone around and when Hanford swung stiffly from his saddle and tried the door, he found it secured against entry with staple and hasp and padlock. A single window cut in the logs to one side of the door was devoid of sash, but solidly shuttered from the inside. At eye height, a brand had been burned into the door with a stamp iron. Peering closely, Hanford ran a finger over it, identifying it as a Running W.

He led the roan around to the stable. Like the cabin it was small, just big enough for two horses. Also like the cabin, it was soundly roofed with heavy, split shakes, which now shed a solid cascade of water. Under that good roof, where the rain was unable to reach, and the drive of the wind was cut off, it seemed almost warm.

Here too, it was virtually dark. Hanford tucked his hands under his arms and rubbed them up and down, warming and drying them. After which he rummaged the contents of one of his saddlebags and came up with a flat tobacco tin. From this he shook a wedge of sulphur matches. He stripped off one, struck it alight on the tobacco tin, nursed it to full blaze and had his swift look around.

There was a manger, half-filled with remnants of wild meadow hay. At either end of the manger was a grain box, licked clean and smooth and dark from vigorous application of eager equine tongues. Hanging from a wall peg was the handle of a rusty old branding iron, the stamp end broken off at the weld. Hanford reached this down as his match guttered out. He hefted the weight of the iron and exclaimed his pleasure.

"Blue, a man can make trouble for himself by breaking and entering, but it's a chance I'm taking."

He circled to the cabin door and set to

work, hammering at the hasp and padlock. He won a little leeway, enough to jam the end of the iron under the hasp and wedge it outward. The hasp bent and he got still better purchase. He gripped both hands around his make-shift pry bar, put a knee against the door and braced to the pull. The staple squealed in protest, then slowly gave. A moment later Hanford pushed the door open.

Cold, but dry air met him as he stepped inside. Several odors of not too distant habitation were there, too, the faint ghosts of bacon grease and tobacco and dried onions. The light of a match located a rough board table, on which was the top of a lard pail holding a half burned candle, held upright by a blob of its own tallow. He touched the match to the wick of this and as the frugal, but sustained glow tapered up, made quick survey of the cabin's interior.

It was, he decided, a line camp cabin, severely plain, holding only the essentials. Yet a welcome shelter on a wild, storm lashed night. At one end was a stove and a fairly well filled wood-box. There was a shelf holding a coffee pot, a frying pan, a couple of stew pots and some tin eating utensils. A bucket stood on the stove and a wash basin and dish pan hung against the wall. A length of cord, strung from wall to wall above the stove, held a dishrag and a couple of passably clean towels.

On the floor against the wall was part of a sack of grain. Next to it was a grub box, its hinged top held shut by a hasp and staple and plug of whittled wood. Hanford explored the contents. There was some coffee, a piece of bacon, some rice, pepper, salt and sugar, some slightly shriveled potatoes and some dried onions that had begun to sprout. Finally there was a bar of soap, a baking powder can stuffed with sulphur matches and half a dozen tallow candles.

At the far end of the cabin, on a length of wire strung to a rafter, a bundle of blankets hung above a wall bunk.

Hanford started a fire in the stove, filled the water bucket under the cabin's streaming eaves, put it on to heat. He scooped grain from the sack into the tin wash basin and carried it around to the stable. The roan whickered anxious greeting and when Hanford emptied the grain into one of the feed boxes, began munching with an eager hunger.

In what was now close to full dark, Hanford unsaddled and lugged his gear into the cabin. He shut the door, fastened the inside latch and let go a long sigh of satisfac-

tion. Let the wind rage and the rain pour —
let the storm do its damndest. For this night
at least, he and the roan were assured of
shelter and food.

He moved up to the stove, added more
wood, then shrugged out of his water-logged
coat. Two small benches were shoved under
the table. He dragged one of these close to
the stove and spread his coat on it. He
whipped the worst of the wetness from his
hat and put it on the bench with his coat.

As he straightened up, his hickory shirt
clung wetly to a muscular back and a pair of
flat, angular shoulders. His hair was thick
and brown, his eyes a frosty gray. The same
angular, big-boned ruggedness suggested
by the weight of his arms and the bulk of his
shoulders, was reflected in a deeply weathered, hard-jawed face. He stood close to the
stove, spread a pair of calloused, muscular
hands to its growing heat. Faintly he began
to steam, and warmth reached through to
comfort and relax.

Outside, the wind had picked up, whining
about the cabin with an elemental rushing.
Rain pounded the shakes of the roof with a
solid fury, and at intervals the far-off mutter
of thunder broke through. A wild, wild
night. And a wet one.

Hanford got a couple more candles from

the grub box, lit them, stuck one on the shelf beside the stove and added the other to the one burning on the table. The water bucket had begun to simmer softly, so he stripped off his belt and gun, hung these on a wall peg, filled the tin wash basin and luxuriated in the feel of hot water. He dried himself with one of the towels hanging above the stove, then got a fresh sack of Durham from his saddlebags, spun up a cigarette and lit it in the candle flame. After which he considered the hunger so alive within him.

He emptied the wash basin into the outer dark, then rinsed the coffee pot under the cabin eaves, and let it fill. Beyond the rectangle of the open door, all was streaming blackness, all wet fury. There was, he mused, a primitive satisfaction to stand in warmth and dryness and taunt the inky elements beyond.

He closed the door, put the dripping pot on the stove and spooned coffee into it. From the grub box he got out the bacon and potatoes and one of the onions. He was searching the utensil shelf for an idea of what it held, when, faint and shredded by the wind, the cry came through the night.

For a moment he thought his ears had tricked him, that what he'd heard was only an extra violent gust of wind shrilling past the cabin. But immediately some inner sense denied this, and he went to the door and swung it wide. Now he was certain, for the cry came again. From over there where the storm-swollen creek charged and battered furiously. A cry that was desperate and urgent. And there was no mistaking the tone.

That was a woman out there!

Hanford drove into the wild blackness, where instantly all was savage resistance. Wind buffeted him, rain drenched him. In his pinched-down eyes was only the utter dark and the sting of chill, driving moisture. He shouted, reaching for an answer. It came from somewhere dead ahead, as nearly as he could tell.

He smashed into a barrier of willows and fought a blind way through the drenching tangle. Branches tripped him, swung from the blackness to lash him across his face. Again he shouted.

Again he got answer, taut and desperate. Close in front of him now, yet below. He fought on through the willows, beating their stubborn clutch. Without warning he broke into the clear and then the earth dropped out from under him and he was sliding steeply down. The next instant he was chest deep in a surging eddy of swirling creek waters.

Barely did he keep his feet, find footing on the boulder strewn bottom. Scant yards beyond was the hungry, racing crest of the creek, now a savage torrent. Where death could easily take a man, once that torrent had him fully.

He twisted, edging a way back toward the bank, fighting the dank, surging flood, leaning and braced against its relentless, treacherous pressure. He reached blindly about, seeking hold of anything that might steady and aid him. Bitter frustration and equally bitter anger whipped him. Now he'd be lucky to save himself, let alone aid anyone else, even should he have located them in this black and wild world.

He could not see the willow branch that hung low across the water, hard bent with the drag of some current swept weight. But his exploring grip settled on it. And stark wonder rocked him. For another hand was clinging there!

He locked his fingers about a slender wrist, and relief charged him with a new and furious strength. He threw a hard call against the rush of the wind and the roar of hungry waters.

"Now it's all right! You can let go — let go — !"

He felt her grip slacken, but when he would have drawn her up to him, found that he could not.

Words reached him, faint and strained.

"My foot — it's caught — a root — snag — something — !"

"Kick!" he ordered harshly. "Kick!"

She did so, twisting, writhing, furiously struggling. Of a sudden she was free, and his pull now brought her close to him. He locked an arm about her and again sought the bank. He reached it and leaned against it while his free hand explored its wet and slippery steepness.

He knew he would need the free use of both hands if he was to have a chance of climbing clear. And he had to make that climb quickly, and not risk sliding back. For the water was plainly rising with every passing moment, the hard pressure of it ever mounting. In the circle of his arm she was so still he thought she might have fainted. He wasn't sure he'd get an answer to his next words.

"I'll need both hands to get us up this damned bank. Can you hang on by yourself?"

Answer was steady.

"Yes. I can do it."

"Good! Get a grip around my neck."

He wasn't sure how long it took him. It seemed he progressed only inch by inch, with every inch a battle. There were root-ends he got hold of, and some of these held and some broke. Where there were no roots he dug his spread and clawing fingers into the soggy earth, and here again, some of this held while some came away in great chunks to slither down into the churning water below.

But the arms about his neck never slackened in their grip, and she had the good sense and courage to be completely still. Even in his moment of extreme effort, Clay Hanford found time to marvel that she should be as she was, instead of full of the hysterics of relief.

He made it finally, with a dragging lunge that topped the treacherous bank and left the thwarted, savage waters fully behind.

"All right," he panted, breath raw in his throat. "You can let go, now."

She slipped down beside him, and so, for a moment, they rested. Then Hanford braced his shoulders against the willow tangle.

"Stay close behind. I'll break a way through."

They came out into the clear of the meadow and Hanford turned and took her arm to aid her. Her step was uneven, limping.

"What is it?" he asked. "Your ankle hurt?"

"I — I lost one of my boots — back — back there in that snag."

He stopped, picked her up in his arms and tramped on to where the cabin door, still open, beckoned its candle glow through the whirling dark. He stepped inside and put her down by the stove, a slim, drenched figure who seemed all streaming, ink-black hair and black eyes in a face drained to pallor. She looked up at him and tried to straighten her shoulders. But abruptly they began to shake. Her lips trembled, her mouth twisted. She dropped her face in her hands and a deep sobbing choked her.

Hanford put his arms around her and held her so as he comforted her gruffly.

"Sure. You've been through a touch of hell. Now, in the relief of knowing you're safe, you got a right to let go."

After a time she quieted and drew away from him. He stuffed more wood into the stove, lifted and shook the coffee pot, which was now giving off steam and rich fragrance. He spoke easily, very matter-of-fact.

"Lucky I put this on the stove just before you called. Get outside of some of it."

19

He filled a tin cup for her and another for himself. As she lifted the cup with both hands, candle light reflected a spark of fire from the diamond on her finger.

Hanford got down the bundle hanging from the rafter, broke it open and shook out one of the blankets. Near one end of this he cut two slits and handed it to her.

"Something for you to wrap up in."

He filled his cup again and carried it to the far end of the cabin. He stood with his back to her.

"All right," he said. "You can get out of those wet clothes."

He waited, lack of sound telling him she had not moved. He turned, reached down his gun from the wall peg and laid it on the table, quick to her hand.

"Any time you think I'm not civilized, use that on me."

He retreated to the cabin's far end again, staring at the wall while rolling coffee's hot goodness across his tongue. Now she was stirring, and to ease the tension he knew must be hers, he spoke casually.

"How did you ever happen to get into that creek in the first place?"

Her answer was muted, subdued, coming in little gusts, as though punctuated by hurried movements.

20

"I'd been — visiting — Alice Lyle. I thought I could — beat the storm home. When I saw I couldn't — I headed here. I saw the open door — someone standing in it — against the light. I thought it was — Abe Kerwin. I didn't realize the creek — could be so high — so quickly. The current — took my horse — right out from under me. I managed to get hold — of that branch. But my feet — were caught — in a snag — or something. I couldn't — pull free. I called for help. You know — the rest —"

"Who is Abe Kerwin?" Hanford asked.

"One of my uncle's riders. You may — turn around, now."

She was wrapped to the chin in the blanket, her arms thrust through the slits Hanford had cut. A blue woolen blouse and divided skirt of tan twill and other odds and ends of feminine apparel hung on the edge of the wood box. A single small boot stood beside the stove.

She had wrung out her hair and it had begun to fluff in the stove's warmth. A little color had returned to her face, and as the candle light struck her eyes fully, Hanford saw they were not black as he'd first thought, but instead a deep, dark violet. Her cheek bones were slightly high, her face tapered. Her chin was soft but definite in contour, her mouth well shaped. Past the rim of her coffee cup she measured him gravely.

"I don't know who you are or how you got into this cabin, for it is usually locked unless Abe Kerwin is here. But I do know there are no thanks large enough to cover what you've done for me."

"Forget it," Hanford shrugged briefly. "Put it that we both had a little luck. I got in the cabin the rough way. I pried off the lock. It was either that or a wet, cold night in the stable with my horse. I liked the idea of the cabin better. If there are any consequences ahead for breaking and entering — well, my back is stout."

"There won't be, though there is a key if you know where to look for it. My uncle owns this line camp. I'm Moira Williamson."

"Clay Hanford, here. How about some more of this coffee?"

She nodded, watching him pour. "Nothing ever tasted even half so good."

"Just you wait a little bit. Supper coming up. Bacon and fried potatoes with onions. And more hot coffee — lots of it. You warm enough?"

"Yes. But you're soaked. Just as wet as I was."

"My boots are full of water," he admitted. "If I get them off the rest won't matter." He touched the gun lying on the table. "If it's all the same with you, I'll put this out of the way."

She gave him a quick, deeply discerning glance, while a tide of color deepened the warmth of her cheeks.

"Of course."

Hanford returned the gun to its holster, went to the door and opened it. He pulled off his boots and emptied them past the sill. Again for a little time he stood, measuring the outer dark with all its elemental violence. Yonder the voice of the creek was a sustained fury, and as it reached the ears of Moira Williamson, she shivered and pressed closer to the stove.

Watching the man at the door she saw him square himself slightly, saw his lips pull thin and the hard line of his jaw become more pronounced. And she knew he was reliving those desperate few moments when hungry waters reached for both of them, and the stark issue of survival or death had been finely drawn. She knew also that here was one to whom rugged conflict of some kind had been a lifetime portion; that he had whipped heavy odds before and was ready to challenge such again.

As Hanford raided the grub box and cooked a simple meal, silence fell, to carry over and deepen while they ate. Moira Williamson wondered at this. Woman-like, she even knew a faint touch of pique. For when, out of the desperate dark his hand had settled about her wrist like some benevolence from heaven, and his strength had pulled her free and carried her to safety, it seemed — illogically perhaps, but with a strong sense of reality — as if in a space of short minutes, she had come to know this man.

It was a feeling that had lasted through his first concern for her comfort and well-being after they had reached the cabin. But somewhere between that time and this, an invisible door had closed, and now, sitting across this rough table from her was a complete stranger, remote in his thoughts and attitude.

The meal, frugal though it was by necessity, was well cooked, and Hanford had been deft and knowing in his preparation of it. Plainly a man, she decided, used to looking after himself. Direct and self-sufficient in every action and thought. But at this moment so definitely a stranger, with his own concerns deep locked behind the frosty gray of his eyes.

The meal done with, she moved to clear

the table. Hanford shook his head.

"Let me. I'll have it done in a jiffy."

Her shoulders stiffened.

"I'm not completely helpless. I've washed dishes plenty of times."

This touch of spirit struck a spark in her eyes and lifted her chin in defiance. The shadow of a smile brushed Hanford's face.

"Sure you have," he soothed. "But you've been through a mighty rough evening. Smart thing for you to do is just rest and let me handle matters."

Aside from her flare of pride, this was easy advice to follow. For though she was now thoroughly dry and warm under her make-shift blanket robe, she was also stiff and sore, and the ankle that had been caught and twisted in the snag, ached dully. Of a sudden she was too completely weary to argue. So she huddled on her bench by the stove, not unlike a tired child.

Done with cleaning up the dishes, Hanford built a cigarette and considered the bunk. The ragged old bedtick was stuffed with dry grass and leaves and was full of humps and sags. He shook this up thoroughly, smoothing and softening it. He spread the rest of the blankets and went back to the stove, his manner and words completely matter-of-fact.

"Now you can get some rest. A long night ahead."

"For you as well as me," she reminded.

"That's right," he admitted. "But I'll get some sleep. First, though, I got considerable drying out to do. So I'll be keeping the stove going."

All the while Hanford cooked the meal, and while he was clearing things away, Moira Williamson had crouched close to the stove, turning her head from side to side, that her hair might thoroughly dry. Now it lay in soft folds, silken, luxurious, ink-black.

She got to her feet and stood looking up at him. Warmth, the security of a sound roof and four stout walls, the inner comfort of hot food, these had proven magic restoratives. Full normal color lay in her cheeks. Despite the weariness that put a faint pressure about her lips, there was in this girl a fine, deep beauty, a bright pride and a quiet courage. These things Clay Hanford glimpsed and recognized. The remote frostiness in his eyes lessened, and he spoke with some gentleness.

"Go ahead. Turn in. I'll guard the fort."

Once again those deeply violet eyes measured him with their searching honesty. Then she nodded.

"Thank you."

26

On bare feet she padded over to the bunk and curled up there under the blankets.

Hanford stoked the stove again, moved in close to it, smoking out one cigarette, then building another. Beyond the cabin walls the storm growled and fumed. Inside, silence took over.

From the bunk, eyes half closed, Moira Williamson watched the man by the stove. His back was to her and again he was that stranger, a thousand miles away. She wondered about him. Where he had come from, where he was going; why the frost in his eyes and why the attitude of distant reserve?

It was not mawkish sentimentality to admit frankly that he had saved her life. This was stark fact. For whatever the blind chance that had led him to her out there in the wild creek waters, certainly it was his strength that had carried her clear. She could never have made it by herself.

Then and later he had been kind and considerate, but in a manner almost completely impersonal. Only once had he seemed to see her as a woman, which was just a moment or two ago. Then, for a breath, his eyes had warmed. Almost immediately, however, a shield of wariness rose in them again.

Drowsily she pondered this. Certainly there was no reason for such wariness, unless he was fleeing from something. Perhaps the law, though somehow she felt this was not so. Far more likely a hurtful memory where some other woman was concerned, so that now her entire sex was suspect. She knew a vague irritation at the unfairness of such a possibility.

Increasing drowsiness clouded her thoughts. Heavier and heavier grew her eyelids. Presently she slept.

Twice more in the next couple of hours, Clay Hanford stoked the fire. Moving with quiet care he brought his boots over to the stove and set them to dry at a safe distance. His clothes steamed and the heat reached through to relax and comfort him physically. Weariness that would not be denied crawled up in him, so finally he put his back to the stove, spread his arms on the table, pillowed his head on them and let weariness have its way with him.

Long later he awoke. The fire had gone dead and a growing chill filled the cabin. The world was quiet. By its own violence the storm had worn itself out. No longer any burly rush of wind, or the pound of rain on the shake roof. Now only the slow, light drip of a few remnants of moisture draining from the eaves, and the distant rumble of the creek.

The candles guttered low, one of them having gone out. But the light of the other two still held back the dark. Hanford glanced at the blanketed figure on the bunk. She had turned to face the wall, and crept deeper under the covers. Her hair lay like a pool of spilled blackness.

An instinct for such things told Clay Hanford that dawn was not far away. So he quietly built up the fire again, rolled another smoke and settled back to await daylight.

TWO

Clay Hanford pulled on his boots, then stood in the open doorway of the cabin and watched the true dawn come in across the timber tops beyond the meadow's edge. Though the meadow itself was still charged with low-lying mists left by last night's wetness, the sky above was clear and flushing rosily in the east. The creek's rumble, though dominant, was muted somewhat to the wilder note it had carried when at full storm crest. From a willow clump a bird called, tentatively but cheerily.

The fresh-washed air was knife keen, vital. Hanford drew it deep into his lungs, welcoming the chill, clean bite of it. All his life he had lived close to the outdoors, and though he had many times fought its more robust elements in their extreme moments, he had always relished them, as they fed a deep lying need in him that nothing else ever reached.

He left the door wide, that this fine freshness might sweep through all the cabin. He stirred up the fire and put the coffee on to cook. After which he went around to the stable to see how his horse was making out.

The roan had a companion, a sorrel filly under empty saddle and with dragging, trampled, mud-smeared reins. Both horses whickered greeting, and the newcomer nosed Hanford's shoulder eagerly. He unsaddled the little animal and returned to the cabin, where Moira Williamson eyed him drowsily from a cocoon of blankets.

"Morning!" he greeted. "I think you're in luck. Sometime during the night a sorrel filly joined my horse. Packing an empty saddle about your size. Does it add up."

She nodded. "Mine. I'm very happy to hear the pony is safe, for it is a favorite. It must have cleared the creek lower down, then came looking for shelter."

"A smart little bronc," Hanford agreed. "Right now a hungry one." He picked up the grain sack. "I'll be outside for a time. Good chance for you to dress."

He divided what was left of the grain between his roan and the filly. While they fed, he used the empty sack to give both animals a rub-down.

When he returned to the cabin, fresh coffee fragrance was adrift and Moira Williamson was dressed. She came around to face him, and Hanford found her clear beauty and the direct impact of those lovely violet eyes definitely disturbing.

"This morning," she announced, "I get breakfast. On that there will be no argument."

He nodded, built a cigarette and stood quietly aside.

Within the hour they were ready to leave. Hanford brought both horses around to the cabin door, saddled them. Minus one boot, Moira Williamson dubiously eyed the soggy earth between her horse and herself. As she hesitated, Hanford, with characteristic directness, picked her up by the elbows and tossed her into her saddle, a display of casual, impersonal strength which left her flushed and breathless.

She wondered at this man's power and the source of it. There was a physical steeliness in him which casual appraisal would never suspect.

He stepped into his own saddle. "You going my way?"

"Which way is that?"

He waved an indicating hand. "There's a town. Morgan Junction. Somewhere out yonder, I believe."

"Yes," she said. "About ten miles from here. Part of the way is my way."

"Lead out," Hanford said.

A trail ran away from the meadow at its upper end, reaching to the northeast, gradually climbing. The sun, high enough now to flood the timber tops, gilded them with a misted fire. Round about, up from the trail and the forest floor, earth's wet odors and flavors lifted in a vital essence.

Despite its rugged experience of the night before, the sorrel filly now stepped out spiritedly and drew Hanford's roan along at a pace which soon left the quick lift of the timbered slope behind and put them on a narrow, little used road running along under the cold shadow of a slabrock rim. Hanford indicated the trace.

"From where — to where?" he asked briefly.

"Ahead it runs into the main Morgan Junction–Hendersonville road," Moira Williamson told him. "West it just fritters out in the timber. It's an old military road. There are a number of such in these hills, many of them about grown over again."

This girl riding beside him, sat her saddle with an easy, supple grace. The soft contours of her face held a composed serenity. Her lips were slightly parted, which, along with her quick bright way of glancing about, told of an eager interest in life and all that it

33

held. Recalling certain desperate moments not too many hours ago, Clay Hanford again silently marveled.

Only once, after he had carried her into the cabin, with the wild, savage breath of the thwarted creek torrent still clinging to them, had she shown the slightest break in a cloak of dauntless courage. And her tears then had been of relief, only.

She reined the filly past the end of a down log that jutted into the roadway. Slanting through the timber a shaft of sunlight struck fire from the ring on the third finger of her left hand. Hanford looked away, vague irritation stirring in him. Another man's woman. The fine ones, it seemed, always were.

They rode east, into the probing lances of a climbing sun, and presently broke into another road. Once heavy with dust, it now was rutted and puddled by the storm, and water lay in wheel tracks recently made.

"The Hendersonville stage, already gone through," Moira Williamson said. "On his out run, Josh Tuttle likes an early start."

They turned left and climbed a winding way through a pass in the slab-rock rim, emerging into clear sunlight on a point overlooking a far-running country. It spread out below them as a land of wide stretches of grass, of timbered, broken ridges which crossed and re-crossed, while, like threads of silver, creek waters glinted here and there.

Clay Hanford needed no second look to know that this was rich cattle country. Grass, water, shelter — all were here, and he understood now the full significance of all old Jess Pinderlee had told him regarding it.

The girl beside him noted Hanford's quick, forward leaning interest.

"Fandango Basin," she said. "Pretty, isn't it? I never pass this spot without stopping for a long look, and always I have the feeling of discovery. As though, like an explorer, or one of the old time mountain men, I was gazing on a pocket of country no white man had ever seen before." She gave a small, quick, apologetic laugh. "Does that sound silly?"

Hanford shook his head. "Not at all. Life would be a mighty dreary affair if we couldn't mix in a little fantasy, now and then."

She studied him with deepening interest. For she had thought that behind those frosty eyes there lay an inner hardness that would deny any of the more gentle conclusions.

"However," he went on presently, "sadly

35

enough, shall we say, men have long been in that basin."

"Yes," she said, her tone taking on a somewhat somber note. "Yes, they have. Perhaps too long. For they've stained it with greed and all the meanness that accompanies it." She hesitated slightly, then voiced the question that had been in her mind ever since learning Morgan Junction was his destination. "I wonder why you are riding into it?"

She saw the shield of wariness lift, and the good moment of intimate reflection was gone. He was the utter stranger again, his answer curt and non-revealing, shutting her out completely

"Business."

With the word he reined away from the point and into the descending run of the road. For a little time she was still, the flag of hurt burning crimson in her cheeks. Then she followed him.

There was no further talk as they dropped down the winding grade to the basin floor below, where shortly a trail broke away from the road past the nose of a little ridge to the west. Moira Williamson drew rein and spoke quietly.

"I leave you here, Clay Hanford. I may never see you again. So, for all that I owe you, and for what they are worth, you have my deepest thanks."

Hanford's reply startled her.

"Back there my manners were rotten. I'm sorry. You don't owe me any thanks. It should be the other way around. For a man can nurse a suspicion until it makes a blind fool of him. And knowing you has made me realize that."

The aloofness in her violet eyes faded, while a dawning smile sweetened her lips.

"That was a very nice thing for you to say, Clay Hanford. Where ever you go and what ever you do, I wish you luck."

With this she would have reined into the side trail, but now a rider broke past the nose of the ridge and came in on them at a driving jog. A fair haired man who sat high in his saddle, with the strong color of a natural arrogance flushing his face. He exclaimed sharply.

"Moira!"

He pulled up beside them and spoke again.

"You couldn't have made it all the way from the Lyle ranch this early in the morning. Don't tell me you spent the night out in the storm?"

"Hardly," Moira Williamson answered. "Not while there is a Running W line camp cabin on Piute Creek."

Behind the newcomer's manner and tone lay an abrupt and possessive impatience. Clay Hanford wondered about this.

The fellow put pale eyes on Hanford, deliberately measuring him.

"Who is he? Where did you meet up with him?"

"At the cabin. Clay Hanford, meet Lute Morgan."

Hanford inclined his head in the barest of nods, his expression inscrutable. Morgan gave no sign of acknowledgement other than a narrowing stare. Then he returned his glance to the girl.

"What was he doing at the cabin?"

"Getting out of the storm, of course. And luckily for me. Else I wouldn't be here."

"Wouldn't be here?"

"Just that. The water was running higher in Piute Creek than I thought. When I tried to ford it, my horse was swept right out from under me. I managed to hang on to a willow branch for a little time. But I'd never have got out by myself. Hearing my call for help, Mr. Hanford found me, hauled me clear, and carried me into the cabin."

Again Morgan's pale glance touched Hanford.

"After that — what?"

38

"Why he loaned me his shoulder to bawl on until I got over being scared. Then I got out of my wet clothes and he raided Abe Kerwin's grub box and cooked a very good supper."

By this time Moira Williamson's shoulders were squared, her head was high, and deepening color burned in her cheeks. Quite plainly she was resenting the tone of this questioning and the obvious direction it was taking.

"Apparently," Morgan said, "a very comfortable night of it was had by all!"

The tone ran a little heavy, a little thick, carrying an inference which the words barely avoided.

Indignance blazed in Moira Williamson, but it was Clay Hanford who answered with swift, cutting emphasis.

"Right! One I'll long remember. And I'd remind you of something, Morgan. Miss Williamson happens to be a perfect lady — and quite a gallant one. While I have my moments of being the complete gentleman. But just now I'm telling you that I don't like what you're suggesting, and I don't like the sneering way you're doing it. You make any more mealy-mouthed talk and I'll shut you up with a gun barrel. Now get the hell out of here!"

Lute Morgan went utterly still. He stared at Hanford with eyes as pale and blank as a cougar's. But Hanford's own frosty glance yielded not an inch.

"You can get out — or argue the point. Make up your mind!"

The ultimatum was as curt, as abrupt as a thrown blow. It was something Morgan had not expected and was not prepared for. There was a gun at his hip, but his mind was locked in uncertainty. For this hard-jawed stranger in front of him was an unknown quantity, and had pushed him badly off balance. The moment was all wrong where Lute Morgan was concerned; it was not his moment and he was shrewd enough to realize it. He tried to modify both his tone and manner.

"You're talking over your head, Mister. Naturally I'm concerned about Miss Williamson. That's my ring she's wearing."

"Misfortune on her part, if true," Hanford retorted. "And doesn't change what I said before a damn bit. Get out of here!"

Very plainly, there were wild fires rioting in Lute Morgan. They narrowed his eyes, they pinched his lips to a thin bloodless line. But they couldn't burn past the ice in Hanford's settled, harsh regard. A strangled ejaculation broke from Morgan's lips. He whirled his horse and spurred to a run along the road to the north.

Hanford watched him out of sight, then considered Moira Williamson gravely.

"What he said — it's true? That's his ring you're wearing?"

She nodded, wordless.

His glance shifted, so that he was looking past her. He seemed to be reaching with his thoughts back to another scene, to another day. When he finally spoke again, there was a note of cynicism running through his words.

"I suppose it makes sense to you. It must, or the ring wouldn't be where it is. But it doesn't make sense to me. For that fellow, Lute Morgan, is no damned good! It sticks out all over him. Anyone would have to be blind not to see that. And you're not blind. So it would seem I've been right all along. There's just no figuring a woman."

He lifted his reins, ready to go. Moira Williamson swung her horse to block his way.

For the past minute she had been staring at him, a little breathless, wide of eye, scarce believing. For she had just seen blaze out of this Clay Hanford a breath of danger so cold and bright it had utterly cowed another man

41

whom she well knew to be hard and ruthless in his own right. Now, however, Clay Hanford had spoken words which whipped a quick flush of resentment through her, and she flared at him.

"Who are you to — to judge me, or my private affairs?"

His regard was inscrutable.

"Who am I to judge? Well, I happen to be the fellow who hauled you out of a wild creek by the scruff of the neck. Not that I'm bragging, understand, or fishing for thanks. It's just that for some strange reason I feel a sort of proprietory interest in you now. I suppose such things happen." He spoke a little absently, as though analyzing something in his mind. "Two people, total strangers up to a certain moment, and through no direct calculation of their own, are thrown together in a situation from which neither emerges quite the same. Either they have lost something, or they have gained something. One thing is certain. They've lived a little time which neither is apt to ever forget, and, whether they like it or not, a certain bond has been established between them. Somewhere in all that, Moira Williamson, you should find an answer to your question."

Again he made as if to leave, and again she

blocked his way. The flush was still strong in her cheeks, but it was not of resentment now. She spoke quickly.

"It would not be wise for you to go on in to Morgan Junction."

"And why not?"

"You don't treat a Morgan as you just did without paying for it. Lute will stir them up. They'll be after you."

"They?"

"The Morgans, surely. And probably some of their friends."

Hanford shrugged, thinly smiling.

"Obliged for the warning. Judging by the color of the one who just left us, there can't be too much to worry about." He touched his hat. "Adios, Moira Williamson. It's been a privilege knowing you. But —" and here his glance dropped to her left hand — "knowing you and meeting him, I just can't figure that ring!"

This time, when he swung the roan, it was with an authority she could not stop. He went down the Morgan Junction road at a swift jog. She stared after him, held with indecision. Then, abruptly, she put the sorrel filly into the side trail and lifted it to a run.

There was no particular shape or plan to Morgan Junction. It sprawled along the flanks of the road at the fringe of a stand of big pine timber. A few of the buildings were solidly built, the rest flimsy, raw-boarded. The heart of the town lay inside a hundred yards. Here was a store and warehouse, a hotel, a stage and freight depot, a saloon and a couple of offices, one of which belonged to the town marshal. Behind this was a log-built jail.

The hotel was the Ute House. The store carried a sign: 'Jos. Gorman. Groceries, Hardware, Gen'l Mdse.' The saloon, somewhat extravagantly, was The Golden. There was a stage and freight corral at the north end of town, where a small ditch of water ran east and west, gurgling through a wooden culvert under the road.

Clay Hanford rode into town slowly, casting his full attention ahead of him. Mainly he was searching for the blaze-faced bay that Lute Morgan had been riding. There were only two saddle mounts in evidence, one in front of the store, the other in front of the saloon. Neither was a blaze-faced bay.

Hanford pulled in at the store rail and stepped on to the scuffed boards of the porch. Hunkered on his heels a yard to one side of the store door was a rider nursing a final puff from a brown paper cigarette. He flipped the butt of this into the street and tipped his head enough to touch Hanford with a swift glance out of bright, wary, black eyes. As Hanford tramped into the store the black-eyed rider shifted closer to the door, head cast a little to one side, listening.

The store might have been any one of a hundred such which Hanford had been in at one time or another. But the man who stood behind the counter and surveyed Hanford carefully, had no counterpart in Hanford's memory. He was startlingly tall, towering inches above Hanford, who stood an honest six feet himself. He was as thin as he was tall, with a long, big-nosed face, and a completely bald dome of a head. His eyes were a hard, squeezed-down brown.

Hanford returned the uncompromising stare. "Gorman?"

Answer was a wordless nod.

"I'll want an outfit," Hanford said. "Blankets, grub, cooking gear. We'll start with blankets. Let's see what you've got."

Gorman shook his head, his voice as thin and reedy as himself.

"No blankets." But when Hanford's searching glance touched a shelf loaded with them, the storekeeper added quickly, "For you, I mean."

Hanford brought tobacco and papers

from his shirt pocket and over the time it took him to build and light a cigarette, kept a steady stare on Gorman, who began to shift uneasily, both body and glance.

"I suppose," Hanford murmured, "you're prepared to say you've no grub or anything else for me, is that it? What happened? Lute Morgan come by and give you your orders?"

Gorman's uneasiness increased. "I got nothing to say," he blurted.

"Different here!" rapped Hanford with sudden harshness. "You heard what I wanted the first time, and you're going to sell it to me."

"No," Gorman retorted meagerly. "It's my store. I do as I please in it. Sell if I want to, don't if I don't. With you I don't."

"Why then," Hanford said, "I guess I'll just have to change your mind!"

"No!" droned Gorman again.

He'd been standing with his hands spread palm down on the scarred, age darkened counter. Now he moved quickly to drop his right hand from sight.

Hanford was faster. He leaned, grabbed, and filled a fist with Gorman's shirt front, high up at Gorman's stringy throat. He set back with a savage pull which brought the gangling storekeeper sharply forward and spilled him belly-down across the top of the counter.

Gorman kicked and squirmed, all bony arms and legs, but was in no position to help himself. All he could do was grunt and curse, both of which he did in great plenty until the pressure of the counter top against his lank middle cut him short of breath.

"Good thing you didn't get hold of that gun you were after," Hanford told him bleakly. "Else I'd have fed it to you, an inch at a time. You going to sell me what I want if I let you up?"

"You'll let him up!"

The voice came from behind Hanford.

He twisted and looked over his shoulder at a stocky man whose seamed face and puckered eyes reflected a wall of harsh, hard wisdom, behind which he stood apart from other men. There was a badge on his shirt front and the bulge of a gun in a shoulder holster under the black calf-skin vest that he wore.

"Yeah," said the stocky man again. "You'll let him up."

Hanford stepped away and the store-keeper struggled erect, breathing heavily through his nose and with a hand pressed to his punished midriff. The man with the badge issued further edict.

"You quiet down too, Joe. Now what's this all about?"

"I want to buy some blankets and supplies," Hanford said. "This fellow refused to sell me any. We argued a mite. Then he reached for a gun." He faced the marshal fully. "You'd be — Challis?"

"That's right — Reed Challis. How did you get hold of the name?"

"I was told." Hanford jerked a nod toward the storekeeper. "You going to back his hand?"

The marshal shrugged. "It's his store. Also, his business any way he wants to run it. You had no call to manhandle him just because you don't happen to like that way."

"I manhandled him because he was going for a gun. You should warn him about that. He could get shot, doing it."

"Maybe," agreed the marshal briefly. "You're lucky he didn't. And you got the look about you of being all smoked up. So the best thing you can do is get out of town."

Clay Hanford had not lost his cigarette during the brief scuffle. But it had gone out. Now he searched for a match, raked it along the counter to set it alight, held it until the sulphur had cooked off it, then brought the clear flame to the tip of his cigarette. Over his cupped hands his eyes gleamed with a cool contempt.

"Morgan Junction," he murmured sardonically, shaking out the match and flipping it aside. "Founded by King Morgan, owned by King Morgan, and run by him and his tribe. Yeah, everybody in the damned town owned by King Morgan!"

Challis eyed him without expression. "That kind of talk won't earn you no favors. What I said, stands. Get out of town!"

"Presently," Hanford replied evenly. "First, I want a talk with you."

"What about?"

"About Fandango Basin and where I stand in it. Because it happens that I own a chunk of it — a real sizable chunk — and I figure to have a voice in its affairs. In short, I'm not a stray saddle bum, to be run out of town as such. Do we talk?"

They measured glances and Challis jerked a shoulder.

"Come on. My office."

At the door, Hanford paused and looked back at the gangling storekeeper.

"I'd suggest you get at least one foot off the Morgan bandwagon, Gorman. Because there are a lot of tomorrows coming up. I'll be around for those supplies later."

Hanford did not wait for any reply, but

49

followed the marshal out and went down the street with him. The shabby, black-eyed rider who had been hunkered beside the door, stared after them, his bright glance full of a quickening excitement. He waited until they turned in at the marshal's office, then got to his feet and sauntered along to the Ute House. Here he settled into a round backed chair, cocked his run-over boots on the porch rail, pulled his hat low over his eyes and lapsed into a watchful immobility.

In his office, Reed Challis took the chair behind the table that served him as a desk and nodded Clay Hanford to a seat opposite.

"All right — I'm listening. It might help if you'd name yourself."

"Hanford — Clay Hanford."

Challis considered a moment, then shook his head. "New to me. And I figured I knew everybody in the Basin who owned any real part of it. Where's your ground?"

Hanford knew he was going to toss a bombshell, but he tossed it.

"My ground is the Reservation range."

Challis had been slouched in his chair. He straightened slowly, his eyes boring at Hanford.

"Since when?" he demanded.

"Since Jess Pinderlee sold it to me. As I

50

recall, the date on the deed reads just a month ago tomorrow."

"I find that a little hard to believe," Challis said.

Hanford shrugged. "The deed is recorded and now in the safe of Jim Ventry's bank in Butte City. And I got a copy of the deed in my saddlebags. I brought it along, just in case some skeptics needed convincing."

Reed Challis settled back in his chair again, dug a stubby pipe from a pocket, packed and lit it. He sucked in two deep inhales before speaking again.

"If this is true, and I expect it is, you've bought yourself more than a chunk of range, Hanford. You've bought trouble!"

"So I understood at the time," Hanford nodded. "When and if it comes, it won't be because I start it. On the other hand, I'll meet it with whatever means necessary. I intend to stand up for my full rights."

Challis fixed him with that remote, measuring glance again, then murmured:

"It'll be interesting."

"What will?"

"Seeing how long you stand."

Outside, the riffle of hoofs sounded along the street, moving in by the Ute House and pausing there for a little time while a hard, heavy voice rumbled. Then the hoofs came on and stopped in front of the marshal's office and the weighty growl of that heavy voice lifted again.

"Challis! Challis — come on out here!"

THREE

There were five riders on the street. Four of them, all men, were bunched in front of Marshal Reed Challis's office. The fifth, a girl, was pulled up at the rail of the Ute House. She had taken off her hat and was hanging it by the throat latch to her saddle horn, and while doing this, watching the group at the marshal's office.

She was fairly tall, her yellow hair parted into two heavy folds which clung to the sides of her head and then gathered in a shining roll at the nape of her neck. She was in divided skirt and blouse of dark blue, with a silk scarf of lighter blue to match the color of her eyes and offer contrast to that corn yellow hair and the strong color in her cheeks.

From where he stood in the doorway of the marshal's office, Clay Hanford noted her presence only meagerly, for his attention was centered on the four mounted men whom Reed Challis now faced. The central figure of these loomed wide and heavy in his saddle — a man strongly grizzled about the temples, with broad, veined cheeks, a beaked nose, arrogant eyes under thatched brows, and a harsh, hard mouth under a down-curving, silver-gray mustache, stained brown from tobacco at the edges.

On one side of him was Lute Morgan, on the other a slightly older replica of Lute, with the same tallness, the same fair hair, the same high coloring in the cheeks and the same pale, arrogant, challenging eyes. The fourth member of the group was a rusty-haired man with a livid scar puckering one cheek.

Reed Challis looked at the older man.

"Something you wanted, Mr. Morgan?"

The older rider did not answer. Instead, he pointed at Clay Hanford and asked growling questions of Lute Morgan.

"That him?"

"Yes," said Lute. "That's him!"

Now the older rider dropped his glance to Reed Challis.

"Thought I told you not to let any of these saddle bums light. This the way you move them out — chinning with them in your office?"

The rough, domineering arrogance of the words made the marshal's shoulders swing restlessly.

"Any man's got a right to be heard."

The older rider switched his hard, uncompromising stare to Hanford.

"You got anything to say — say it to me!"

"Be glad to." Hanford moved out beside Reed Challis. "You, of course, would be King Morgan, head of the Morgan clan. Heard about you. Heard a lot about you. Jess Pinderlee told me."

King Morgan came a little higher in his saddle.

"Jess Pinderlee! Where did you know Jess Pinderlee?"

"Met him in Butte City, at Jim Ventry's bank. Had chance for a long talk with him while Jim Ventry fixed up the deed and all the other angles of the deal."

"What deal?"

"Why," said Hanford crisply, "the deal on the Reservation range, here in Fandango Basin. I bought it from Jess Pinderlee."

If this word had been a bombshell when Hanford gave it to Reed Challis, it was now doubly so. The rusty-haired man with the scarred face mumbled profane surprise, while King Morgan swayed far forward in his saddle, and if the weight of the stare he put on Clay Hanford had been fire, then Hanford would have instantly shriveled. King Morgan exclaimed with gusty anger.

"I don't believe it!"

Hanford shrugged. "It's signed, sealed and in the records. You might as well get used to it."

King Morgan folded both hands on his saddle horn, pushed himself back and fully erect again. The veined color in his cheeks became a livid stain.

"Jess Pinderlee never rightfully owned the Reservation range, so how can you?"

Hanford shrugged again. "You're trying to talk against and deny fact, Mr. Morgan. The government sold that land to Jess Pinderlee — gave him clear title to it. Now that title has been transferred to me. Also tied in with the deal is the little item of some two hundred J P Connected white faced cattle. These, as I locate them — and wherever I locate them — will be vented to my own Rafter H iron, which has been duly entered in the brand register at Butte City. And if those two hundred head — give or take a dozen — are not to be found in Fandango Basin, I'm going to ask some damned embarrassing questions and insist on some straight answers. I hope we understand each other, Mr. Morgan?"

King Morgan had a son on either side of him, and now the elder of these spoke up, as hard and uncompromising as was his sire.

"You keeping on making that kind of talk and you won't be around long enough to get any answers at all!"

"That'll do, Price," growled his father. "I'll handle this." He fixed his heated regard on Clay Hanford once more. "Something for you to understand. The grass on the Reservation range was always held as joint property of men who rode this basin long before either you or Jess Pinderlee ever heard of it. Pinderlee wasn't able to use it, and you won't either!"

"I'll use it." The frost was beginning to pile up in Hanford's eyes. "At one time Reservation grass might have been free grass. Not now. Now it's my grass. And if you got any cattle grazing it, move them off. Else I will!"

King Morgan's words fell harsh as stones.

"Big talk — oh, very big talk! Fight talk! Well, here is my word to you. You want fight — you'll get fight. Yes, you'll get your fun!"

"If I have to fight, it won't be fun," Hanford told him evenly. "For there is no fun in the way I fight — no fun at all!"

As though consumed with some restless, angry impatience, Price Morgan was swaying from side to side in his saddle. Now, despite his father's earlier admonition, he bought in again.

"You talk like you held all the aces in the deck. This might be a good time to have a look at them!"

Nodding to his brother Lute, he reined a little to one side. Lute hauled his horse the other way. Both watched Hanford with a fixed narrowness.

Reed Challis tossed an abrupt hand.

"Easy — you two! Don't try and start anything!"

Price Morgan's answer might have been the lash of a whip.

"Why, damn you, Challis — would you be forgetting who your friends are?"

"Maybe I'm wondering about my so-called friends," Challis said bleakly. "You heard me — easy does it!"

Now it was the elder Morgan who put the full power of his florid stare on the marshal, as if, by the sheer weight of it, he would crush all resistance. But Challis gave not an inch.

Watching closely, missing no move or shade of expression, Hanford glimpsed the faintest break in King Morgan's over-bearing certainty. This touch of doubt carried over into his words, weakening them of their impact.

"Have you grown proud, Challis — a little proud?"

Challis shrugged. "I quit being proud a

long time ago. But I still carry the badge. I'm telling Price and Lute not to start anything they can't finish!"

"That's making it pretty plain," King Morgan said.

"That's how I meant it to be," Challis said.

King Morgan reined his horse half around and looked at the roan-headed man with the scarred face.

"Mitch, it's time to hold another meeting. You get the word to Buck Siebold. Price, you hunt up Frenchy LeBard. Lute, you get on out to Running W and tell Hack Williamson to come in. I'll be waiting for them in the Ute House tonight."

Price Morgan was prepared to argue, but his father, bruskly harsh, cut him short.

"Do as you're told!"

Mitch, the scar-faced one, left town without a word. Price still hesitated, jerking his head at Reed Challis.

"How about him — now that he's gone proud?"

"Among other things," King Morgan promised, "we'll talk about Challis."

Price and Lute headed out together. King Morgan folded his hands on his saddle horn again and tipped his heavy shoulders forward.

"Yes, Challis — we'll get around to talking about you."

The cattleman swung his heavy stare to Hanford.

"While you," he growled, "you'll be gone from this basin before tomorrow morning if you know what's good for you. Neither you or anyone else is moving in to push aside those who opened this country and made it good. My final word — leave now, or never!"

With this, the cattleman reined away to the Ute House, got down and tied, then stamped, heavy heeled, up the porch steps, paying no attention to the black-eyed, shabby rider in the round-backed chair, who, to all intents and purposes, was fast asleep under his low tipped hat.

His glance following King Morgan, Clay Hanford saw that the girl with the corn yellow hair had left her saddle and was standing on the hotel steps, idly slapping a pair of buckskin gloves against the palm of her left hand.

She said something to King Morgan, who paused a moment to answer. Then, as he tramped on into the hotel, she turned and with long, indolent strides came along the street, her glance frankly curious as it sought Hanford.

In her was the strong Morgan family resemblance, the fair hair, the high coloring. Also, even the challenging arrogance of the Morgan stare, though here it carried an added insolence.

As she passed, Reed Challis touched his hat brim in a purely automatic way, but he might as well been a stone for any attention the girl paid him. All her interest was on Hanford, and, while he held her gaze fully, it was with a reserved indifference which made her shift her glance and put a stronger beat of color in her face. Her step quickened and further along she turned into Gorman's store.

"That," Hanford murmured, "would be — Lear Morgan?"

Reed Challis nodded. "Pinderlee must have given you a pretty complete picture?"

"On some things," Hanford admitted. "Like the Morgan family. On you, too."

"Like what you saw, just now?" The marshal's words were tight with bitterness.

"Part of it," said Hanford. "Where you told them off."

The marshal's laugh was biting, mirthless. "I surprised myself. I'm wondering why I did it."

"I think I know. What a man really is, deep down, sooner or later shows up."

Hanford looked toward Gorman's store. "I still need that list of supplies and gear. You any objections to my getting them?"

"Not now," Challis said. Then he added with vehemence, "no objections at all. You got the money to pay, go get what you want. And if Gorman plays stubborn, bounce his belly on the counter again!"

Saying which, Town Marshal Reed Challis wheeled toward his office door. He paused a stride short of it, slowly turned.

"I hope you listened to the last thing old man Morgan said to you?"

Clay Hanford tipped his head. "I listened."

"Good enough," Challis said. "Just so long as you realize he meant every damn word!"

"I know he did. I meant what I said, too."

"That you'd fight — and there'd be no fun in it?"

"Yes."

Reed Challis brooded for a moment, then shrugged. "I think you're a fool to try. But good luck!"

Heading back to Gorman's, Clay Hanford pondered the abrupt change in attitude by Reed Challis. It did not surprise him too much. For Jess Pinderlee had told him that in his opinion Challis was basically a sound man, who would, some day when the weight of dominating Morgan arrogance became too heavy, turn on it. Apparently, Hanford decided, such a turn had begun.

In the store, Lear Morgan was talking to its proprietor. Conversation broke off abruptly and both turned to face Hanford when he entered and moved up to the counter.

"If you're waiting on the lady, Gorman — go ahead," Hanford said. "I'll wait my turn."

Gorman cleared his throat and spoke with his nasal drone.

"I told you there was nothing in this store for you."

"That's right, you did," Hanford conceded. "And I said I'd have to change your mind on that point. I thought perhaps I had. If not, I'll have to start again where I left off when Challis showed up. Only, this time he won't show up. In fact, he told me to come and get what I want. It was all right with him."

Joe Gorman's Adam's apple ran nervously up and down his stringy neck and he looked away.

"Listen, man," Hanford said, his tone smoothing out, "I don't want to quarrel with you. This is straight business. You got the stuff I want — I got the money to pay for it. In the future I expect to buy plenty out of this store."

Joe Gorman looked from side to side, his expression that of a man caught in a trap, or squeezed between two forces. His glance, when it did settle, was on Lear Morgan.

"You see?" he burst out, almost accusingly. "I got no choice. You tell your father that." He looked at Hanford. "I ain't fixing to make no fight of this. Long as you can pay for it, you can have what you want."

"Fine!" Hanford said. "We'll start with blankets."

Lear Morgan drifted a little to one side and watched Clay Hanford select his gear and supplies and stack them on the counter. Her expression was one of baffled uncertainty, mixed with a quickening pique. For the cool indifference with which this wide shouldered, raw-boned stranger treated her presence was something new in her experience. In the past her usual problem had been, not to awaken men from indifference, but in most cases to rear a barrier against their too-eager interest.

She was a graceful girl and a pretty one, despite the air of insolent arrogance with which she surveyed the world and all those in it. Besides, she was King Morgan's daughter, the apple of his eye, and pretty much the accepted first lady of this wild, lonely basin land. To win her favor was to win King Morgan's favor. Yet, here was this tall, lean-flanked rider showing no more interest in her than if she were one of the brooms stacked in yonder corner.

Basically, despite her pose of arrogance, and almost sensual air of insolence, Lear Morgan was even more child than woman. Brought up in a household of men, spoiled to death in her own home, and fawned upon outside it because she was who she was, her view on life had inevitably become somewhat lopsided, self-centered and, to a degree, selfish. This was the lingering child in her. While the woman was the sum of all the ripening mental and physical stirrings battling to break free of these more juvenile bonds.

Clay Hanford rolled his blankets compactly. Into an empty flour sack he sorted enough cooking and eating utensils to meet his immediate frugal need, and into another he put some food supplies and a caddy of Durham. He spun a golden double eagle on the counter and grinned without malice as Joe Gorman counted out his change.

"Old Blue, my bronc, is liable to resent all

this stuff hung on him. Figure I'm making a peddler's horse out of him."

Gorman did not answer.

Hanford lugged his purchases out to where the roan dozed hip-shot in the sunshine. Except for a thin, cottony roll of clouds touching the far crest of the hills here and there, the sky was all a clear, shining blue. Drying, the street steamed in the sun's direct warmth.

Hanford tied his blanket roll behind the cantle, and the two sacks to his saddle horn, one on each side. Blue swung a suspicious head and rolled a wary eye.

"I know," Hanford murmured. "Your pride is all hurt to hell. But don't go getting any wringy ideas, else you and me will fuss. And, as usual, you'll get the worst of it."

He went into the saddle, swinging a high leg to clear the bulk of saddle-bags and blanket roll. From this eminence he had another look along the street. Only one person was in sight. The shabby, black-eyed rider was still on the hotel porch, but he had left his chair and was leaning indolently against one of the porch posts, spinning up a cigarette. In this small chore he seemed completely absorbed. As Hanford rode past, heading north out of town, the shabby one showed him no direct glance, but under a shadowing hat-brim, black eyes showed an ever heightening glint of excitement.

When the timber lanes lining the road north of town drew Hanford from sight, the shabby rider lit his newly fashioned smoke, dropped off the hotel porch and sauntered along toward Gorman's store at a leisurely, spur-jangling gait, as if completely indifferent to anything but his own idle thoughts. He loosed the tie of his pony at the store hitch rail, hooked the near stirrup on the saddle horn and tightened the latigo a trifle. After which he dropped the stirrup, put a toe in it and lifted to the saddle. As he did this, Lear Morgan came out of the store.

The rider eyed her approvingly.

"Lear, like I told you before, you blind my eye. You grow prettier every day."

She tossed her head. "If my father or brothers heard you say that —"

"Sure," he broke in. "Just the idea of a saddle tramp like me daring to speak to you is enough to bust an artery in every male member of the Morgan family." He went quickly on, his words touched with a thin bitterness. "But it wasn't always so. While Tap Timberlake owned a piece of range they wanted, it was quite all right for him to know you, to ride with you and visit with you, and even speak you sweet. But now that they got him elbowed off that range, it's to hell with Tap Timberlake. Now they're waving you in front of Buck Siebold, a man twice your age and two-thirds gorilla."

She flared hotly. "That isn't true, Tap Timberlake. I — I'm not being waved in front of anybody. Just — just because Buck Siebold and Dad are good friends —"

"I know," cut in Tap Timberlake again. "I thought I was a friend of the Morgans — once. So did Frank Billings. Now we're just a pair of saddle tramps, sleeping in the jack pine thickets, riding the fringe trails, out at the knees and elbows and with run-down boots. While Crown cattle grow fat on grass we once grazed."

Again she denied him. "That's not so! Neither you or Frank Billings was ever able to really use the grass you claimed. And — and grass belongs to the man who can use it."

Young Tap Timberlake eyed her through a moment of sober appraisal. His shabby clothes were badly worn, faded and fringed. His cheeks were grubby with unshaven whiskers. Yet, beneath these the planes of his lean young face were clean and hard, and his black eyes were clear and direct with a dogged honesty.

"They've trained you well, haven't they,

Lear? Even got you saying it now. That grass belongs to the man who can use it. How many times have I heard a Morgan say that! And always as justification for pushing another man out of his lawful rights. Like they did me. Like they did Frank Billings. Like they'll do Buck Siebold when they get ready to. According to the Morgans, the only people who can use grass legitimately, are the Morgans."

She stamped a foot. "Tap Timberlake, you're saying terrible things! Why — you'd make my father out a — a — !"

"A damned old pirate! Which is exactly what he is. And one who has spoiled so many things for so many people." He lifted his reins, but held his horse steady. "Like he did for us, Lear. Remember the fun we used to have — you and me? Remember the rides we took and the rainbows we chased? You used to laugh then, Lear — with your head back and your eyes shining. Like a lovely happy kid. How long since you've laughed that way, Lear — how long?"

Young Tap Timberlake shook his head with a sort of gentle regret, spun his horse and was gone.

Lear Morgan stared after him, the color of her anger fading slowly from her cheeks. Her eyes held a big stillness, and there was no insolence now in the turn of her shoulders or her slim young body. Now was only a softening about her lips, and a trembling. And her head was bent as she hurried back to the Ute House.

Some two miles above town, Clay Hanford left the road, reining into a lesser, but fairly well traveled trace which angled to the northwest. This, according to directions Jess Pinderlee had given him, was the way into the Reservation range.

It was a pleasant way, skirting between low timber ridges here, then breaking out across stretches of open grass, to presently again thread past another low, timber-dark ridge. Last night's storm had sweetened and enriched all this land, and a little wind, running here and there, was keen and cool, and carried, from the timber depths on these low ridges, the good scents of resin and damp forest mold, and on occasion the faint, shy fragrance of some delicate woodland bloom.

He reached a fork in the trace and kept to the right hand one, which, a little further along, charged straight at a ridge, climbed it, crossed it, and from the far side dropped down into a wide running sweep of grassland dotted here and there with little clumps of timber and cut through from northeast to southwest by a willow-fringed water course.

Hanford pulled in the roan while he had his good look. A quickening gleam shone in his eyes and a smile that held something of almost boyish eagerness, momentarily softened the lines of his face. For this land he was now looking down upon, was his. This was the Reservation range.

There were cattle on it. Here and there he saw them, grazing in the full open, moving along the creek, or resting at the fringe of some timber clump. Huddled against the creek was a cluster of buildings. Once these had been the headquarters of the military. Now they would be his.

He rode directly for them, marking the brands of the cattle he passed along the way. The musing half smile faded slowly from his lips. For, while he read Crown — lots of Crown, and Long S and Tin Cup and Sixty Six, and two head of Running W, he saw not a single critter carrying the J P Connected iron.

He came up to the headquarters layout, stepped down and looked around. At a distance he had thought these to be fairly solid buildings. But this closer survey showed that time and the elements and the neglect

71

of long disuse had worked their usual inexorable way. In addition to what had been the larger of the military structures, several weather-grayed cabins crouched about. Also, there was an old corral in the creek meadow. Hanford unsaddled and turned the roan into this.

The cabin that looked in best repair stood somewhat apart from the others. Hanford lugged his gear over to it and pushed a way in. The door protested loudly on its rusty hinges, but swung clear. There was a window and only one pane had been knocked out of the sliding sash. The roof had successfully resisted last night's wild onslaught, and, decided Hanford, no sterner test would ever have to be met.

In here there were definite signs of not too distant occupancy, for the stove, though battered and rusty, held ashes and cold cinders of fairly recent burning. There was a bench that had evidently seen service not only as such, but also as a table. And against one wall was a roughly constructed bunk.

With the bulk of the day still ahead of him, and what he could probably salvage from the other buildings, Hanford figured to have things in pretty fair shape by sundown.

He beat this goal by a full two hours, and

with hunger alive and gnawing in him, built a fire in the stove and put on his coffee and bacon to cook. Shortly after, the muffled thump of hoofs drew him to the cabin door.

The rider was the shabby one who had been hunkered in front of Joe Gorman's store and who later shifted to the porch of the Ute House. In town, Hanford had noted his presence only casually, seeing him as someone completely outside his own particular interest. Now, thinly alert, Hanford took another and closer look.

The rider's glance was open and steady, his grin wryly cheerful.

"Timberlake, here," he said. "Tap Timberlake. Heard you tell King Morgan that you'd bought this Reservation range. Thought you might need a hand, while I need a job. Also, the whiff of that good coffee and bacon is pullin' me like a coyote to bait. Yeah, friend — I'm panhandling a meal. But," he added, sobering, "I figure I can pay you back in a lot of ways."

Hanford did not answer immediately. In his time he had climbed some pretty tough trails which had left rough scars, and made him wary of men and their ways, and armored him with a certain taciturn skepticism. However, he was not a sour man, nor yet a complete cynic. And the direct, open-faced approach of this young rider appealed.

"Light," he said briefly. "Grub's near ready." On impulse he added, putting out his hand, "Hanford — Clay Hanford."

In one of the other cabins he had found a rickety table. In another an equally decrepit bench. He had repaired and strengthened these and brought them to his own use. Now he faced Tap Timberlake across the table while they ate.

"If you heard what I told King Morgan, then you must have heard what he said in return. He aims to make me open game. Were you to ride with me you'd be in the same class — open game. A man's got only one life, Tap. There's no profit in giving it to protect another man's interests."

Tap shrugged, reckless bitterness gleaming in his black eyes.

"If I can help bust King Morgan some way, then I'll be serving my interests as well as yours. By myself I got no chance. Riding for you, I have."

"What is it you have against the Morgans?"

"Like this," Tap said. "I'm the last of my family, but my folks were among the first in this basin. They settled on the north fork of May Day Creek and put in plenty of work and hardship in getting a spread started. Our range was mighty valuable because it gave access to a considerable chunk of government land, further back along the base of the Greystone Hills. Well, King Morgan took to playing up real friendly for a time, offering to pay me so much a head for any Crown beef I'd let cross my land to graze that far back government grass.

"At the time I needed money more than I did the government grass, so I agreed. I never saw a cent of the money, and the first thing I knew, Crown cattle were thick, not only on the government grass but were all over my May Day Creek range, too. When I put up a howl, Morgan just laughed at me and asked me what I was going to do about it." Tap shrugged. "There wasn't a damn thing I could do. I was a lone man against the Crown outfit."

"You join me, there'll just be the two of us," Hanford said. "What makes you think we'd stand any better chance?"

"I heard the way you stood up to King Morgan. I heard the way you threw it right back in his eye. You got the look about you. You got rawhide in you. You're the kind of man I been waiting for to show up in this basin. And I want to tie in with you and see it through, regardless! If you're interested, there can be three of us."

"Who," Hanford asked, "would be the third?"

"Frank Billings," Tap said. "And one hell of a good man. Older than you or me, but tough and steady, the kind you can depend on plumb to hell and back. Also, yearning night and day for a chance to kick a spoke out of King Morgan's wheel."

"What did the Morgans do to him?"

"Burned him out. He had a cabin over on South Fork. He ran a few head, just enough to keep him in groceries and tobacco. He didn't ask any more than that — just to be left alone to mind his own business. But the Morgans wouldn't let him. He owned a little grass and they wanted it. So — they burned him out."

"You sure? Burning a man out is pretty raw business."

Tap Timberlake shrugged. "You don't know the Morgans. They just don't give a damn. Nobody's got any rights but them."

"There are other ranchers in the basin," Hanford pointed out. "What about them?"

Tap's lips curled in contempt.

"If you mean Buck Siebold and Rusty Acuff and Frenchy LeBard, they're just the tail to the Morgan kite. They hang along with King Morgan and what he tells them to do, they do. Some day when he's ready to, he'll push them off the earth, too."

"I heard of another," Hanford said. "Man named Williamson."

"Hack Williamson," Tap said. "Owns the Running W. A good man with wire in his spine. Minds his own business and stays pretty much away from the rest. There's one angle about the Williamsons and the Morgans I can't quite figure, but it's none of my business. All I know is that when Morgan and the others put the big push on Jess Pinderlee to run him out of the basin, Hack Williamson never mixed in the affair at all. He wasn't for or against anybody; just played it neutral."

Hanford cradled his coffee cup in both hands, looked at Tap across the rim of it.

"You figure you can locate this Frank Billings?"

Tap nodded quickly. "Sure of it."

"What's this angle between the Williamsons and the Morgans you can't figure?"

Tap squirmed, looked uncomfortable. "I like the Williamsons. Hack, his Missis, and Moira, Hack's niece. I consider them all my friends and I wouldn't do or say anything, ever, that might hurt them. So — what's none of my business is none of my business."

"Would the fact that Moira Williamson wears Lute Morgan's ring be the angle you don't savvy, Tap?"

Tap's eyes widened. "How'd you know?"

Hanford smiled faintly. "I knew. I can't figure it, either."

"Then suppose we forget it?" Tap said gruffly. "None of my business — none of yours. Moira is one swell girl."

"Sure she is," Hanford agreed, his smile widening. "Tap, you're all right. You'll do to take along. How soon can you get hold of Frank Billings?"

"Might be some after dark, time I get back with him."

"Good enough. Just remember, both of you, there's damn little I can offer you at first but trouble — big trouble and lots of it. The odds will be heavy and the going rough. Think it over."

"I have," Tap said grimly. "I know how I feel. I know Frank Billings feels the same way."

"Which settles that," Hanford said. "I may not be here when you return. I'm going into town again and it may be late before I get back."

Tap, on his feet and heading for the door, stopped abruptly, turning.

"I ain't trying to tell you your business,

understand," he said. "But was I in your boots, I'd stay out of town tonight."

"Why?"

"King Morgan is calling a meeting. You heard him. At the Ute House. They'll all be there. The Morgans, Acuff, Siebold, Frenchy LeBard, Hack Williamson —"

"And me," cut in Hanford. "I'll be there, too."

"But — but — hell, man," stuttered Tap, "you're the cause of the meeting. King Morgan aims to hang your hide up to dry if he can. You know that. No sense in asking for it. Town will be crawling with people who won't like you."

"Fine!" Hanford said. "Give me a chance to know them, next time I run into them. Remember, Tap — I'm a Fandango Basin cattleman myself, now. So I've full right to sit into their meeting."

Tap stared at him, then shrugged.

"Maybe you're right. Maybe your way is the way to do it. Brace the whole damn bunch, look 'em in the eye and let 'em know exactly where you stand and where they stand."

"It's been done," Hanford said meagerly. "All I know is — damn few fights were ever won, backing up."

Tap Timberlake considered this,

shrugged again and went out. Shortly the mutter of departing hoofs ran away into silence across the creek meadow.

FOUR

In the deepening dusk Clay Hanford caught and saddled and made ready for town. He had washed and shaved and from the depths of his well-stuffed saddlebags, donned a clean shirt. Also, from the saddlebags, he had taken a folded paper of heavy legal bond and stowed it carefully in a pocket. He did not buckle on his gun, instead tucking the weapon in the waist band of his jeans, well around to the left side, under the flap of his faded denim jumper.

With the closing in of full dark, chill settled over the world and the early stars glowed big and bright. Hanford rode with some wariness, testing the night ahead of him. Only once did he raise sound of anyone else abroad but himself, which was after passing the forks of the Reservation Road, when the echo of fast trotting hoofs and the skirl of iron shod wheels came faintly back to him.

Coming into town his wariness deepened. Light glowed yellowly in the Ute House, in the Golden, in Marshal Reed Challis's office, and in Joe Gorman's store. A number of saddle mounts lined the hitch rails of the Ute House and the Golden. A buckboard and team stood in front of Gorman's.

At the far end of the same rail, beyond the out-flare of any light, Hanford tied the roan. Now that he'd have Tap Timberlake and probably another to feed besides himself, he turned into the store to order up another sack of supplies. Joe Gorman was stacking some purchases on the counter in front of a middle aged couple. At Hanford's entrance Gorman looked past his customers, started slightly, stared, then dropped his glance.

Off to Hanford's right, low exclamation sounded.

"Clay! Clay Hanford!"

He came around to face Moira Williamson.

Her skirt was of light tan corduroy, and over a blouse of the same material and color, a buckskin jacket was snugly buttoned against night's chill. Tucked about her throat was a scarf of yellow silk, and against this, her hair, glinting with a blue-black lustre under the lamp-glow, made strong contrast. Her eyes, so deeply violet, carried their usual disturbing loveliness.

Hanford went gravely still, his glance intent.

Color beat up her cheeks and she laughed softly, but with a touch of uncertainty.

"I'm the usual me," she assured him. "Just looking a little less like a drowned rat than the first time you saw me."

Hanford drew a deep breath, then murmured:

"It's hard to believe!"

"What is?"

He shook his head, locking back the thought that had occurred to him.

Now concern sobered her.

"You shouldn't be here, you know. There's a special meeting going on because of you. Clay, it's true — you bought the Reservation range?"

"Yes. From Jess Pinderlee. And I'm looking in on that meeting. As legitimate owner of range in the basin, I figure I've a right to attend. That's reasonable, isn't it?"

She studied him for a grave moment.

"I'm not sure whether it is or not, under the conditions. But I do know it is like you to do it. Your way will ever be your way. Now I want you to meet my folks. I know they want to meet you."

She turned to the couple at the counter.

"Aunt Molly — Uncle Hack — this is the

man. This is Clay Hanford."

Hack Williamson was all cattleman, weather-darkened, saddle-leaned, solid of feature and with quick, blue eyes. His wife was buxom, gray haired, pleasant faced. It was she who spoke first, and impulsively.

"Moira told us all about last night, Mr. Hanford. It is hard to find words for the gratitude we feel."

"None needed, ma'am," Hanford said. "Like I told your niece, we were both lucky."

Hack Williamson's handshake was firm.

"Molly said it for both of us, Hanford. I'm glad to know you."

"My privilege, sir," Hanford replied.

A man called from the street.

"Hey, Hack! They're waitin' on you. And Morgan's all of a fret!"

Hanford saw a gust of angry impatience sweep through Hack Williamson, and equally angry retort form on his lips.

"Someday I'm going to tell King Morgan — !"

His wife stopped him with a swift touch on his arm.

"Some day, Hack," she said gently. "The right day. Go along, now. You don't have to do a thing but listen."

The cattleman turned to Hanford. "Did I hear you tell Moira you were going to the

84

meeting? Come along with me."

Hanford shook his head.

"Wouldn't be fair to you, Mr. Williamson. If we walked in together, that could damn you completely in the eyes of some. Not that I don't appreciate the offer, understand. I'll show, later."

Hack Williamson gave him a moment of keen scrutiny, then nodded.

"I'll be looking for you."

He went out, a quick stepping, sure striding man.

Lank and towering, his bald head shining under the down pouring light of the lamp, Joe Gorman considered Clay Hanford with a new and grudging respect.

"Something you wanted?"

"I'll wait my turn," Hanford answered.

Molly Williamson spoke quickly. "Don't mind Moira and me. We're in no hurry. We've no place to go and nothing to do until Hack gets back. Go ahead, Joe — wait on Mr. Hanford."

Gorman put his glance on Hanford again. "Well?"

Hanford named off his mental list. "Sack it for me. I'll pick it up later." He turned to Moira and her aunt. "Thank you, ladies!"

Moira walked with him to the door, and as he stepped through into the dark beyond, called softly.

"Luck, Clay. And — be careful!"

She had used his name naturally, and her concern was genuine.

They were gathered in the barroom of the Ute House. Rusty Acuff, Buck Siebold, Frenchy LeBard and Hack Williamson occupied chairs. Price Morgan and Cob Jacklyn, foreman of the Crown outfit, stood at the bar, whiskey glasses in front of them. On the far side of the bar, handy for further service, was the moon-faced, heavy-bodied proprietor of the Ute House, Mike Scorry.

King Morgan stood facing the others, his feet spread and his hands gripping the back of a chair, his shoulders swung forward in their usual cast of heavy, overpowering belligerence, and he was just ending a growling harangue.

"— we didn't stand for Jess Pinderlee taking over our grass, and we'd be fools to let this fellow Hanford light and get dug in. I say we should stop him right in his tracks. I want your opinions on this. Buck?"

Buck Siebold was stocky and broad, with long, heavy arms dangling from sloping shoulders. His facial features were heavy to coarseness and his brows and hair almost cotton-light. He was just as heavy mentally as he was physically, and just as shambling. Whatever King Morgan said at any time about anything, was good enough for Buck Siebold. He blurted his assurance now, and Hack Williamson eyed him briefly with thinly concealed contempt.

In turn, roan-headed, scar-faced Rusty Acuff and Frenchy LeBard echoed Buck Siebold. Frenchy LeBard was almost cadaverously thin, very swarthy, with eyes that always fumed faintly in their far depths, as though some banked inner fire burned there, never completely extinguished. A dangerous man, so the word had it.

King Morgan looked at Williamson.

"Hack?"

Williamson had lighted a cigar. Now he rolled this in his lips, took it out and surveyed the slightly ashed tip.

"Afraid I can't go along with you," he said slowly. "I think we are faced with the inevitable and that it is high time we recognized it and accepted it."

"What do you mean?" asked Frenchy LeBard. "What is this inevitable?"

"Why, that the Reservation range is no longer free grass," Williamson said. He went on quickly, to head off rising argument. "Sure, I know, you fellows ran Pinderlee out. You might do the same with this fellow Clay Hanford, which would seem a simple chore on the face of it, for he's just one man. But maybe he's not as solitary as he seems. Maybe he's got outside backing that's big and strong and can swarm in here and —"

"Maybe — maybe!" broke in King Morgan. Throwing an impatient hand back and forth in front of him; a characteristic gesture, as though he would brush aside all opinion save his own. "That's mealy-mouthed talk, Williamson, and you know it. Pinderlee was big business along side of this fellow Hanford. And we handled Pinderlee all right."

"Jess Pinderlee is an old man with property and ranching interests scattered across three states," retorted Hack Williamson. "My feeling is that Jess Pinderlee bought the Reservation range more as a speculation than anything else. Oh, sure — once he had it he threw some cattle on it, but his heart was never in putting up too much of a fight for it. With Hanford, it could be a lot different."

"But you're not concerned too much, either way, are you Williamson?" said Frenchy LeBard thinly. "You never helped us against Pinderlee, and you won't against Hanford? Is that it?"

Hack Williamson shrugged.

"Long as you ask, no — I won't. Because I never could see any sense in fighting against the inevitable. And if another man owns grass, I accept the fact that I have no right to it. It's as simple as that."

"If he owns it?" put in Rusty Acuff. "If he does? King here, he's noway convinced that this Hanford has any legal claim to the range at all. I go along with him."

"Then," said Clay Hanford, "you're wrong, too!"

He had come into the hotel quietly, and been standing unnoticed at the barroom entrance long enough to hear most of the last comments. Now he moved on down the room, hooked an elbow on the bar and stood leaning there while his glance ran slowly over the group.

Price Morgan pushed away from the bar, squaring himself.

"You got a hell of a nerve! Nobody invited you here."

"Invited myself," Hanford said curtly. "And it doesn't take any special brand of nerve to walk into a public bar. And this is such, isn't it?" He flicked a glance at Mike Scorry. Without waiting for an answer, he made another brief survey of the gathered cattlemen.

89

"I won't take too much of your time." From a pocket he drew the legal paper he had folded and stowed there. He shook it out and handed it to Hack Williamson. "Mind looking that over and telling the rest what it says, Mr. Williamson? There seems to be some who question my ownership of the Reservation range, and I want to convince them otherwise. This paper is a true copy of the deed of ownership."

Hack Williamson took the paper, hitched around in his chair a little so the light of the hanging lamp struck more fully. Hanford rang a coin on the bar. "A couple of your best cigars," he said to Mike Scorry.

Mike Scorry showed a moment or two of uneasy reluctance, then pushed a half filled box along the bar. Hanford selected two, pocketed one, lit the other and looked through the smoke at Hack Williamson, who now returned the glance, then swept the others with a slow survey. He tapped the paper with his finger.

"It's all here," he said slowly. "Description of property, proscribed boundaries — everything. Based on exact government survey. And it states that full title and ownership is transferred from Jesse J. Pinderlee to Clay Hanford for —" and here Williamson spaced his words with a distinct emphasis — "for the consideration of one silver dollar, United States coinage!"

Momentary silence held, then King Morgan lunged forward.

"Let's see that!"

He jerked the paper from Williamson's grasp, scowled over it, reading swiftly. His head came up and he charged furious words at Clay Hanford.

"You expect me to believe a damned old skinflint like Jess Pinderlee would sell you — or any other man — all that grass for a single dollar? On the face of it, this thing is a fake!"

Price Morgan stepped up beside his father, claimed the paper and glanced at it.

"Of course it's a fake. Just like you, Hanford. Get out — before I run you out!"

He tore the paper in half and threw the pieces in Hanford's face.

"You shouldn't have done that," Hanford said softly.

He stepped in behind a driving fist. Price tried to dodge, but was not fast enough, catching the blow full in the mouth. It drove him into a card table, over which he floundered, half stunned. Hanford grabbed him, swung him around and threw him against the bar. Bouncing off this, Price met another clubbing blow that dug deep into the side of his neck, under his ear. He went down in a sprawled, loose heap.

It had been fast, very fast. Hanford faced the room again.

"You see!" he told King Morgan harshly. "I warned you there'd be no fun in the way I fight. And this can get rougher. If you want it so!"

They were held through a long moment of immobility. Then Frenchy LeBard hit his feet and Buck Siebold followed. Cob Jacklyn swung away from the bar. King Morgan stared at Hanford, switched his glance to Price's sprawled figure, then brought it back to Hanford again. The cords of his throat were distended. His words fell, thick and heavy.

"Yes! Yes, it can get rougher. It will! Cob get over to the Golden and pass the word to the boys. This fellow Hanford doesn't leave town alive!"

Hack Williamson came up fast, protesting. "No! I won't stand for that. Price asked for what he got. You can't —"

Frenchy LeBard cut him short. "Keep out of it, Williamson! This is between the rest of us."

At this moment Town Marshal Reed Challis walked into the room through the arch which led to the foyer. Cob Jacklyn had started to leave. Challis caught him by the arm, spun him around, headed him back.

"You're not going anywhere just now, Cob."

The marshal's glance traveled on, to touch Price Morgan, who, now stirring, rolled over and pushed up on one elbow, dazed and stupidly staring. Challis looked at Clay Hanford.

"Maybe you shouldn't have hit him. Then again, maybe he shouldn't have acted the way he did. I'm calling this even."

He turned to King Morgan.

"From in there —" he nodded toward the foyer, "I looked and I listened. Now I am having my say. This thing stops right here! You give any orders calculated to get somebody killed, I'll hold you strictly responsible. That understood?"

Turgid blood gathered in King Morgan's face, congesting behind his eyes, giving them a bloodshot look.

"Challis," he said ominously, "I think you better turn in that badge!"

The marshal shook his head. "Later, maybe. Not now."

"Yeah, now!" put in Frenchy LeBard.

Challis turned on him and Clay Hanford clearly saw the gust of antagonism which leaped up, raw and savage, between the two

93

men. It was not a thing of the moment, but something far older. It reached back to an earlier day, to some previous time when these two had clashed over an issue.

"LeBard," Challis said flatly, "get out of town!"

"In my own time — my own time." Frenchy LeBard's shrug was open taunt. "First, we'll take that badge off you!"

Bleak light formed in the marshal's puckered eyes and he walked straight at LeBard.

"All right," he said, dangerously soft, "you've made your talk. Let's see you take off my badge!"

In Frenchy LeBard a flicker of startled uncertainty showed. He measured Reed Challis carefully and backed up a step.

The marshal's lip curled. "Like I thought. Face to face you're all talk. You do your shooting when a man's back is turned."

He threw the words with a vast contempt, going steadily forward. With every step he advanced, Frenchy LeBard gave way a step. So they moved out of the barroom into the foyer, with dark fury ever mounting in LeBard, but also ever retreating before the cold menace in the marshal.

"Get out of town!" ordered Challis again.

At the hotel door LeBard blurted a curse, whirled and lunged out into the night.

Challis came back into the barroom. Price Morgan had struggled to his hands and knees. Cob Jacklyn reached down an aiding hand and hauled him upright. Price leaned against the bar, limp-legged. His head and shoulders sagged, and a slime of blood ran down his chin from his battered mouth.

Clay Hanford looked around, spoke in cool, curt tones.

"I think we understand each other." He turned to Reed Challis. "All right with you if I drift?"

"All right, yes."

Hanford had a last word for King Morgan. "You leave me alone, I'll leave you alone."

"That," said Challis, "is a very reasonable statement. Think it over, Morgan."

Hack Williamson fell into step with Hanford, and Challis, after a blunt, hard look at King Morgan, followed. The three of them stepped into a night that was big and chill. Stars were far away in a velvet sky, yet let down a certain glittering degree of silver light.

To the men with him, Hanford said: "Morgan won't like either of you for this."

"Hell with Morgan!" Hack Williamson stated flatly. "Right now I'm not caring a damn what any Morgan thinks or doesn't think. Challis, I liked the way you handled Frenchy LeBard. Far as I'm concerned, you can be the marshal of this town for the next thousand years."

"We'll see," Challis replied enigmatically.

They paused in the light flare at the door of the marshal's office. Challis dropped a hand on Hanford's arm.

"Ride light and careful," he warned. "In this town I can keep an eye on things. But I've no authority beyond it."

"Obliged," Hanford nodded. "I'll remember."

Out of nowhere he knew a quick liking for this man Reed Challis. He drew the spare cigar from his pocket and presented it.

"A fair smoke — on me."

He and Hack Williamson went along. Reed Challis nipped the tip off the cigar and scratched a match against the door post. He got the cigar alight and savored the fragrance of the smoke as it curled smoothly across his lips.

Over in the deep shadow at the corner of the Golden Bar, a brief stab of gunflame showed, and report rolled hollowly along the street. A heavy slug smashed into the back of Reed Challis, knocked him to his knees.

Somehow he came back up, grabbing for support at the door post with one hand, reaching for his gun with the other.

From the shadows the feral gun pounded again, and a second slug hit the marshal, angling through his chest. This one brought him down, limp on his face, half in, half out of the doorway of his office.

When the first shot sounded, Clay Hanford and Hack Williamson were just about to move on to the porch of Joe Gorman's store. They came around and saw Challis reeling and weaving in the doorway of his office. They saw him jerk under the impact of the second slug, and they saw him go down.

"It's LeBard!" exclaimed Hack Williamson. "That dirty, treacherous bastard!"

He headed back at a run to the marshal's side.

Hack Williamson carried no gun this night, and it was a tribute to the basic courage of the man that he go as he did to the aid of Challis. To make certain that Williamson reached Challis, Hanford drew his gun and laid two quick shots into that pocket of blackness at the corner of the Golden.

An answering slug, winging a little wild, thudded into the store wall at Hanford's back. He threw a third shot. And now, from somewhere up by the far end of the store, two other guns bought in, not at Hanford, but instead picking at the area by the Golden. Out of that area a darting figure raced, low crouched through the thin light beam from the saloon window, found shelter among the rearing, half-spooked saddle mounts crowding the Golden's hitch rail.

Abruptly one of the horses whirled into the clear, rider just rising to the saddle. The two guns beyond the store sent the echoes sailing across the night once more, and the horse went down in a wild, flailing fall. The rider, not yet firmly in the saddle, kicked free, landed stumbling, went down, got up and ducked back among the horses at the rail. A moment later he came out of the tangle again, low in the saddle on another mount, spurring this one to an immediate dead run and reining it sharply off the street into the black safety of an alley.

From where the two guns had blared, came a low, anxious hail.

"Hanford — Clay Hanford! You all right?"

"All right," Hanford answered. "Who — ?"

"Timberlake and Billings. We located your horse and been waitin' for you."

"Stay there," Hanford called. "I'll be along."

Men were boiling out of the Golden and from the Ute House. Hanford slid his gun back under his jumper and hurried to join Hack Williamson, who was down on one knee beside Reed Challis. There was no stir, no move by the marshal.

"Dead?" Hanford asked.

"Stone!" Hack Williamson's voice was tight with quiet fury. "This is murder, Hanford — low down, shoot-in-the-back murder! Whatever Reed Challis called LeBard, it wasn't enough."

Men gathered about the horse that was down in the street. Others crowded about Hanford and Hack Williamson and the dead man lying at their feet. King Morgan came pushing through this morbid circle. He stopped and stared, and Hack Williamson answered his unspoken question with bitter emphasis.

"Your fine friend LeBard did this, Morgan. A sneaking coward from the dark. He shot Challis in the back!"

Price Morgan, moving up at his father's side, mumbled past his split and swollen lips.

"Maybe it was LeBard. If it was from the dark, how do you know for sure?"

From the street a man called, "This is LeBard's bronc."

"LeBard's horse?" blurted King Morgan, finally finding voice. "How — why — ?"

"I told you how," Hack Williamson said. "LeBard was hid out over by the Golden. He did his shooting from there. As to the why, ask yourself and give an honest answer."

"That's where the shootin' started," agreed someone in the crowd. "I was in the Golden and the first shots were right outside the south corner of the place."

Another echoed this observation, adding, "Somebody else did some pretty good shootin', too — downin' Frenchy's horse."

"Could have been me," Hanford said harshly, though knowing quite well that it wasn't. For he wanted to keep the part of Tap Timberlake and Frank Billings out of it. At the same time it was his mood just now to accept any challenge.

"What you got against LeBard?" called someone from well back in the crowd. "What did he ever do to you?"

"He just killed a friend of mine," Hanford retorted, his glance searching for the speaker, but with no success.

Lamplight from the open door touched those of the pressing, curious group, struck up the hard shining of their eyes. Some of the eyes showed expressions frankly hostile. Others were guardedly neutral. None were openly friendly.

Hanford turned back to Hack Williamson.

"Who takes care of all the necessities in cases like this?"

Before Williamson could answer a husky Irish voice took over.

"The town will take care." Moon faced, rotund bodied, Mike Scorry pushed to the front. "Ay, it will be as I say. For he was a good man and he belonged to the town."

Hack Williamson said, "Thanks, Mike."

The hotel owner shrugged, looked at Clay Hanford. "A pity your lead did not find LeBard, instead of his horse. Now, if you'll but lend a hand — ?"

The three of them carried Reed Challis into his office, laid him carefully on the floor.

Mike Scorry reached down a coat from a wall peg and spread it over the marshal's face and upper body, while speaking with surprising gentleness.

"Yes, he was a good man. Far too good to die at the hands of the likes of Frenchy LeBard."

From the doorway, King Morgan said:

"Is that any way for you to talk, Mike?"

"I said it," stated the hotel owner flatly. "I meant it. And I will stand by my words!"

He shouldered King Morgan aside and tramped solidly out. Morgan stared after him angrily, then came around to fix Hanford with his hot stare.

"All this — because you came pushing into this basin!"

"No!" Hack Williamson differed emphatically. "All this because of you and that God Almighty pose of yours. Telling everybody else what to do. Denying the rights of other men because such rights don't agree with your own damn selfish ideas. This is your fault, Morgan — all of it!"

Morgan's stare switched to Williamson.

"Now," he said, heavily sarcastic, "you're going proud on me. First it was Challis, then Mike Scorry. Now you. Hack, I'd be a little bit careful?"

"Which I intend to be," was Williamson's curt retort. "It's that kind of place now, Fandango Basin is — a place where it pays all men to be careful. Which includes you, Morgan. Now, a final word. Where I and mine are concerned, you will mind your own business completely. You and yours will stay away from me. You will stay off Running W land. Until this night I'd had only a partial look at you. Tonight I saw it all. And I just don't care for what I saw. Am I understood?"

The characteristic surge of turgid blood congested King Morgan's face again and his eyes took on their bloodshot look.

"We'll see," he charged thickly. "We'll see!" He whirled and went out.

Clay Hanford stirred restlessly.

"To a degree he was right. This did happen because of me. And I'm damned sorry about it."

Williamson shook his head. "Not your fault. All you did was to hasten something that was bound to happen. This basin has been edgy for a long time and steadily getting worse, because of the weight the Morgans have thrown on it. Once I thought it might be possible to live with them without bending the knee completely. I've found that couldn't be. So now I've had my full say to King Morgan, and I feel better for it."

So saying, Hack Williamson put out the lamp and they left, closing the door carefully behind them. All along the street men were swinging into their saddles. A considerable group headed north from town.

"Crown," said Hack Williamson. "The Morgan outfit."

Other smaller groups broke away here and there. Hoofs trampled and the echoes of men's voices ran back and forth. Then the mutter of hoofs was gone and the sound of voices gone, and the street lay empty and silent.

In the out-pour of light from the door of Gorman's store, a slender figure showed, then turned back in.

"Moira," said Hack Williamson. "She and Molly are fretting. With good reason. I better hurry along."

At the store, Williamson turned in. Hanford went on past into the thick shadows beyond and found two figures waiting him there beside his horse.

FIVE

It was pushing midnight when Clay Hanford,
Tap Timberlake and Frank Billings rode in
at the old Reservation headquarters. They
had lingered in town just long enough to
watch Hack Williamson guide his women
folk from Gorman's store, put them in his
buckboard and drive off into the night. Then
Hanford went in and claimed and paid for his
sack of supplies which Gorman had put up.

He was prepared to tie this to his saddle,
but when Tap Timberlake and Frank Billings brought up their mounts from the
dark, Billings had a pack horse at lead, carrying a meagre outfit. They added the sack
of supplies to this load and headed out.

The ride home through night's steadily
deepening chill had been without event.
Now, while Tap and Billings unsaddled
and corraled the horses, Hanford went into
the cabin, lit a couple of candles, started a
fire in the stove and put on a pot of coffee
to cook.

Tap and Billings had blanket rolls of their

own, which they brought in and spread on the floor.

"Be a little rough on you boys, sleeping there," Hanford said.

"Just for tonight," Frank Billings said briefly. "Tomorrow I'll knock together a couple more bunks."

Back in the darkness of town, when Tap had introduced Billings, Hanford's impression had been of a thin, frugal-worded figure with a handclasp that was lean and sinewy. Now, touched with candlelight, Frank Billings showed as a still-faced man with deep set, shadowed eyes and gaunt cheeks frosted with grizzle.

Hanford waited until the coffee had turned over and they were sitting at the table, nursing steaming cups of it. Then he put the proposition bluntly to Frank Billings.

"I'll be happy to have you along, but I can't promise you a damn thing but trouble. Sure to be, for a time. Later, maybe, with a lot of luck and some damn fast scrambling, we may do better. I've already told Tap that was the way it was sure to be, and I want you to understand the risk thoroughly, too."

Billings gave a small shrug. "All I want is another chance at the Morgans, along with a little company. Alone, a man can't do too much. But with a couple of others, maybe he can do a lot."

"It could be open season on the three of us," warned Hanford. "In the Ute House tonight, King Morgan was set to issue orders to his men that I was not to leave town alive. He didn't get away with it then, because Reed Challis stopped him. Now they've killed Challis, and there is nothing to stop Morgan from spreading the word. He may do it."

"He will do it!" Frank Billings said. "For he is that kind. It is rule or ruin with him. He doesn't give a damn who he pushes around, or how. He's made arrogant, top-heavy fools of his two sons. Lear, the daughter, is a pretty sound girl, deep down, but the old man is squeezing her to death, too, with his damned overbearing pose of authority. Given time, the Morgan family will fall apart like a tree with a rotten core. But before it does it can hurt a lot of people."

"It already has," put in Tap Timberlake. "You and me, Frank — we ought to know."

"There's more," Billings said. "There's Reed Challis and Jess Pinderlee."

"I could know tears for Reed Challis," Hanford said. "For he was a good man who had just found himself. But I'd never waste any over Jess Pinderlee. From what I've seen, there's damn little to choose between him and King Morgan. This you probably didn't know. Jess Pinderlee sold me this Reservation range for one dollar."

"One dollar?" Tap burst out.

"That's right — one dollar!"

"But — but — man alive — that don't add up," sputtered Tap. "This range — for just a single dollar! What — why — ?"

"To get even," Hanford said drily. "That's all. Just to get even. King Morgan called Pinderlee a skinflint, and he didn't miss it far. Pinderlee has long had more money than he'll ever need in his lifetime. Being run out of Fandango Basin the way he was, galled him, plenty! But at the same time, he didn't cotton to the idea of what he could cost him if he tried to fight his way back in again. And with no assurance of success, it could add up to a case of throwing a lot of good money after bad. So, he tried to sell title to the range for just what it cost him. Nobody, it seemed, wanted it, not at that price or any other. For they knew that along with the range, they'd be buying the same fight Pinderlee wanted no further part of."

Hanford drained his cup and twisted up a smoke.

He lit this by tipping his head over one of

the candles. He drew a deep inhale and went on.

"I'd done several jobs of work for Jim Ventry on range properties his bank had acquired. I happened to be present the day Pinderlee was there, trying to talk Ventry into buying the Reservation range. Jim said he wasn't interested. Pinderlee kept dropping his price lower and lower until Jim told him flatly he wouldn't have it as a gift, not with the fight sure to go with it. Pinderlee stamped around and vowed if he could find anybody willing to go into Fandango Basin and make an all-out fight of it, he'd deed them the range as a gift. I figured the ornery old devil was just sounding off to get rid of his mad, and for the pure hell of it, I called him. I told him I was his man. Damned if he didn't take me up on it!"

Hanford got to his feet, took a short turn up and down the cabin, his face cast in somber speculation. He put his back to the stove, spread his hands to the warmth.

"To simplify the transfer of title I paid him a dollar, which made it a legal sale. So now you know how it happened. Jess Pinderlee, before he is anything else, is a damned good hater. He wasn't spreading any benevolence my way. Far from it. There's no real benevolence in him. He was just taking a long gamble that I might be able to move in, make my claim and make it stick. If I did that, then, in a sort of left-handed way, he could feel he'd got even with King Morgan and the others who helped run him out of the basin. And should I meet up with a slug, then I'd be the dead man, not him. And he'd just write off what he'd already lost, anyhow."

Tap Timberlake wagged his head, still dazed.

"So much — for just one dollar!"

"So much, but in more ways than one," reminded Hanford. "There's the fight that goes with it, remember. But I went into this thing with my eyes open. I knew the odds I'd have to buck. Any smart gambler would back away from a ten to one bet on it. However, as things stood, I wasn't getting anywhere in particular with the job I had, and, though the risk to my hide would be greater, moving in here wasn't too different in principle to what I'd been doing. I'd just be fighting for my own interests, instead of the bank's, and if I put it across, I'd have a real start toward an outfit of my own. It would mean the reviving of an old dream. So — !" He shrugged. "You fellows still interested?"

"We sided you in town," Frank Billings said. "If we'd had any doubts, we'd have stayed clear then."

Hanford nodded. "Fair enough. We understand each other. We put this thing across, I'll make it right with you."

"All I want is to get back what I had before," Billings said.

"That's it," put in Tap. "For me, the old home place on May Day Creek. My folks are buried there. It's where I was born."

"Both of you had cattle, of course?" Hanford asked.

"Some," Billings told him. "And we still got a few, back in the big timber country over west, in the foothills behind the old Scatone ranch. Tap and me been siwashing it out there, keeping an eye on things."

Hanford took a final drag on his cigarette, opened the stove and dropped the butt into the coals.

"According to what Jess Pinderlee told me, there was a considerable number of J P Connected strays he didn't have a chance to gather when he pulled out of here. He said any I could locate I could regard as mine — as part of the deal. They were lost to him, and he didn't want the Morgans or any of their good friends to benefit. So, I'll be looking for those strays, and any I find, I vent to my own Rafter H iron, right then and there. I told King Morgan as much."

For the first time the taciturn mask of Frank Billings showed a break. A shadowed grin creased his gaunt cheeks.

"One way or another, friend, you sure stirred things up. For a fact you did."

"I wouldn't give a damn," Hanford said, "if only Reed Challis was still alive."

"That Frenchy LeBard," said Tap Timberlake. "There is a bad one."

Harshness swept across Hanford's face.

"I'm looking forward to getting that fellow right in front of me, when I'll whipsaw him until he fights or crawls."

"He'll crawl," Frank Billings declared. "Oh, he'll snarl and sneer and hate your guts with those crazy eyes of his, but he'll still crawl. Then wait for his chance when your back is turned. Like he did with Challis. For what you may figure it's worth, Hanford, I'd offer this advice. You ever get LeBard in front of you the way you want, make him go through with it. Make him fight. Don't let him back down. No matter how he backs and crawls and evades, make him see it through. Because if you don't, if you let him slide out on you, then he'll be lookin', day and night, for the chance to back shoot you."

Frank Billings was never more deadly serious, which Hanford realized.

"You wonder how even Morgan can stand a fellow like that around."

Billings tipped a shoulder. "Because he's some useful to Morgan, that's why. The day he ceases to be, Morgan will step on him just like he would a bug. Make no mistake about King Morgan. Basically, the only difference between Morgan and Frenchy LeBard is that LeBard does his own bushwhacking, while Morgan gets somebody else to do his for him. Don't ever look for mercy in King Morgan. You'll never find it. And remember what I say about LeBard. Tap called it. He's a bad one."

"Too bad you and Tap didn't get him instead of his horse."

"We tried. Yes — we tried!"

"How did the pair of you happen to land in town?" Hanford asked. "I told Tap to wait out here for me."

"That's right, you did," said Tap. "But Frank and me, we talked things over, and having a fair idea of what you could run up against in town, decided we better swing by and have a look see, just for luck. Out here, we wouldn't have been no good to you."

"No," admitted Hanford gruffly, "you wouldn't have. I'm glad you showed."

"Tomorrow," Tap asked. "What's in the cards for tomorrow?"

Hanford yawned and stretched. "We'll see what sunup brings. Until then, we'll sleep on it."

Sitting the buckboard seat between Aunt Molly and Uncle Hack, Moira Williamson was glad of the warmth afforded by their protective shoulders, and by the blanket she and Aunt Molly had wrapped about themselves. For this night held a chill that was not all of climate.

After that ragged burst of gunfire along the street of town, there had been anxious moments for Moira and her aunt where they waited in Joe Gorman's store. Anxious until Uncle Hack had come in. Afterwards came the shock of learning of the violent death of Town Marshal Reed Challis at the hands of Frenchy LeBard.

Knowing her Uncle Hack thoroughly, Moira could read the cold anger which consumed him. She and her Aunt Molly were silent in the face of it. They heard his brief immediate explanation of the shooting, then carried their purchases out to the buckboard and headed homeward under the cold stars.

That more lay behind her uncle's mood than just the shooting affair, Moira was certain, and she knew her Aunt Molly was

equally sure of it. But both waited for Hack
Williamson to give them all of the picture in
his own good time. It came with a blunt declaration.

"Molly, I've broken with the Morgans!"

Moira felt her aunt stir slightly. Then, in-
finitely wise and patient and understanding,
Molly Williamson gave quiet answer.

"You must have felt you had to, Hack."

"I had to!" Hack said tightly. "I'd taken
all I could. Lord knows I've tried to find
some basis of reasonable agreement with
King Morgan. But Molly, there's no getting
along with a Morgan unless you bend completely to their will. And that I will never do!
I'm not entirely sure King Morgan isn't
mentally unbalanced. For the man seems to
have delusions of personal grandeur. He
would be omnipotent. He would give life or
take it away. Tonight, because this newcomer, this Clay Hanford, refused to be
bullied or bluffed and because he demanded his lawful rights, King Morgan was
going to order him killed!"

"Oh, Hack — as bad as that!" Aunt Molly
cried softly.

"As bad as that! And it led directly to the
other affair. Because Reed Challis heard
Morgan make the talk and called him on it.
At which, Frenchy LeBard bought in,

taking up for Morgan. Challis ordered Le-Bard out of town, made him crawl. For that, LeBard waited in the dark and shot Challis in the back."

Aunt Molly was still for a moment. "I'm afraid, Hack," she said simply. "A thing like this can — can reach so far, strike at so many —"

"Unless it is headed off," agreed Hack tersely. "But I refuse to drag my self-respect in the dirt any longer, just to hold some show of favor with the Morgan family. So I laid it on the line with King Morgan. I told him I wanted no further part of him or his, that from now on all Morgans were to stay off my land, and that —"

"Hack! You're forgetting!"

There was a little stretch of silence, and then Hack, speaking gruffly, said:

"I guess I did, on that angle. I'm sorry, Moira."

"You mustn't think of me, Uncle Hack," Moira said quickly. "You did what you felt you had to do. I understand, perfectly."

They rolled along without further talk. Moira's hands were tucked under the robe. She felt the ring on her finger — Lute Morgan's ring, and her thoughts ran back over the chain of time and circumstance that had placed it there.

Lute — one of the Morgan boys. Tall, fair, good looking. And the land was far and lonely, and there was the call of youth to youth. Also, a girl's dream of romance. Lute could be good company, was good to look upon, and owned, when it pleased him to show it, a certain charm. Moira had known a certain fondness for him, though she had never tried to consciously gauge the full measure of her feelings until the time when the ring appeared.

It was a day when Lute, visiting, stayed for supper. Afterward, she had walked out with him to where his horse waited. There he had told her to close her eyes and hold out her hand and see what fortune might bring her. Believing it all just a bit of light teasing, she had done as he asked. When she opened her eyes the ring was on her finger, with the pale glow of the stars building a spark of glinting fire in its jeweled heart.

"I sent clear East for that," Lute had said.

It had surprised her, confused her, left her uncertain until the moment to consider immediate return of the ring had passed. Then had come further cause for surprise and confusion. Lute had pulled her close and, despite her instinctive resistance, kissed her long and hard. After which he was swiftly in his saddle and on his way into the night, leaving a parting remark ringing in her ears.

"You're all mine now, Moira!"

Immediate reaction had been a bewildering admixture of emotion, made up of some excitement, some anger, and a faint touch of fear. Even the opinion of her aunt and uncle was lost in the first overwhelming rush of bewilderment and uncertainty. Since then they had neither openly objected or openly approved, adopting an attitude of reserved waiting.

That was how it had been at first.

Long since had Moira reached the conviction that she could not continue to wear Lute Morgan's ring. She did not love Lute and now knew she never could. For, since viewing him in a new-found critical light, she saw in him several things that troubled her and that she did not care for.

There was, too close beneath the surface, a certain wildness, a lack of stability. Also, now that she wore his ring, there showed an increasing arrogance, a will to dominate, and an air of possession which left her with ever deepening resentment.

"You're all mine now, Moira —"

The words had come to haunt her.

Since claiming her lips that first and only time, he had attempted several times since to claim them again, only to go off into long spells of sulky anger when denied. It was, Moira knew, exactly as Uncle Hack had said. To get along with a Morgan you had to be subservient.

So she knew that one day she must return the ring. And she knew Lute Morgan's arrogant pride was certain to make the moment a highly disagreeable one. Viewing with distaste this inevitable unpleasantness, she had, humanly enough, postponed it as long as she could. Too, she had clearly understood her uncle's attempt to stay on some degree of friendliness with the Morgans, which was another reason for her own reluctance to act.

Now that particular reason no longer existed. Uncle Hack had broken completely with the Morgans, wanting no more of any of them, even to the extent of denying them passage over his land. So she, too, must now face up to the necessary move, despite the unpleasantness certain to follow. The next time she saw Lute, Moira now vowed silently, she would return his ring.

These were her thoughts and conclusions and her decision as she mused, made drowsy by the steady skirling of buckboard wheels and the measured clop-clop of trotting hoofs. Just as drowsily, she listened to her uncle's words when he finally spoke again.

"It could be, Molly, the Morgans have met their match. If you had seen the way Clay Hanford cut Price Morgan down to size, you'd know what I mean."

Moira straightened, instantly wide awake. Silently she echoed Aunt Molly's startled question.

"Cut Price down! How do you mean?"

"With his fists," Hack Williamson said. "Price asked for it. He tried some of that usual damn Morgan arrogance on Hanford. It didn't work. Hanford hit him just twice and Price ended up on the floor, about as badly messed up from two punches as any man I ever saw."

"That will set them after Mr. Hanford, of course," Aunt Molly said. "They'll never rest until they feel they've got even."

"They'll be after him," agreed Hack. "But whether they find him in the spot they want him, is something else again. The man's no fool. He's smart and he's tough. Maybe entirely too tough for the Morgans to handle."

"It's a pity," said Aunt Molly softly. "All of it. How much simpler it would be to live and let live. Why can't men understand that?"

"Some men do," said Hack. "But there are always others like the Morgans."

Aunt Molly considered a moment. Then:

"How will it affect us, Hack? I had hoped to never see you again reach in anger or need for that gun and belt which hang on the wall of your room."

"There's no telling just how it will affect us," Hack said slowly. "I managed to keep clear of the Morgan-Pinderlee fuss. Maybe, by minding my own business, I can keep out of this. I'll certainly do my best to. But if I have to lay aside my self-respect, to lay aside the gun, then it comes off the wall once more. A man can only do what he has to do, Molly."

Between Uncle Hack on her right and Aunt Molly on her left, Moira Williamson huddled a little lower and shivered, not from the chill, but from the shadow of a dark foreboding which now seemed to fill the night.

SIX

Carrying his saddle, Clay Hanford tramped from cabin to corral and stood for a moment, facing the morning glow pouring past the crest of the Greystone Hills. Lower down, on the flank of the hills and along their base, shadow held, deep and cold, but out here in the wider run of the basin, sun's first strong touch wiped out shadow and laid broad bands of golden fire across a wakening world.

Flavors and fragrances, brewed during the night, swelled from the earth. Yonder, creek water made its ripple and its splash, and birds twittered and sang and flitted busily among the willows. From some high eminence a hawk's cry carried down, thin and wild.

The color in Hanford's cheeks, the light in his eye, quickened. Lifting all about him was an invisible something which stirred him, in mind and body. It took a little time to identify this vitalizing intangible. Then, of a sudden, he knew. Possession! That was it — the strong sense of possession!

For this land he stood on, the broad acres stretching away on every hand to certain distant limits — these things were his. Signed, sealed, deeded, recorded. His for so long as he might live, if he were strong enough to hold them. Only death could rob him of them.

Events of last night came sweeping back, clear and sharp. Slowly the exultant light left his face and eyes. The one grew harsh and reserved. The other took on a fixed, gray chill, and he moved to catch and saddle. For there was much to do and the fates allotted a man only so much time for the doing.

Tap Timberlake and Frank Billings came up, eyed Hanford questioningly. Understanding, Hanford said:

"I've a fair idea of the limits of my range, but I'd like to get the picture a little more definite. Either of you know my boundaries?"

"I can come pretty close," said Tap.

"Good enough. It might be a good idea for one of us to stay close around. Such as it is, this will have to be our headquarters for a time, so why risk having someone sneak in and touch a match to it?" He looked at Billings. "You mind, Frank?"

Billings shook his head. "Give me a

chance to fix up things around the cabin."

Tap led the way, north across the creek. Clear water foamed and sparkled about the legs of their horses.

"Fandango Creek," Tap identified. "Rises in a big spring up by Reveille Gap then angles down and west through the basin and out through Lyle Canyon. Fine water the year round. King Morgan's been watering Crown cattle along this creek for a long time and he doesn't want to give up an inch of it. Now me, if all the Fandango Creek trout I've eaten were placed end to end — !" Tap grinned.

There was, Clay Hanford decided, a mixture of quick-spirited appealing boyishness and the cynical bitterness of an adult in Tap Timberlake. He knew, however, that in Tap and Frank Billings, he had come up with two staunch, reliable supporters. This they had already proven.

Reservation range north of Fandango Creek was much the same as south of it. A land of scattered, low, timbered ridges with grassy meadows winding between. Here too, as south of the creek, were cattle; Crown, Sixty-six. Long S and Tea Cup. But nowhere any sign of J P Connected.

"Pinderlee," observed Hanford, "could have been lying."

Tap's head came around. "Lying about what?"

"The strays I mentioned. So far I haven't seen sign of one."

"Maybe," said Tap significantly, "you haven't looked in the right place."

"Where would that be?"

"Come up here and I'll show you."

Tap hauled out of the meadow and up one of the timber ridges. At the north end of this they broke into the clear. Tap reined in and pointed.

"That busted up country way out yonder is the Smokies. Part of it is Frenchy LeBard country. Swinging east, it runs into Buck Siebold. Between the two of them they just about control all the north end of the basin, west of the Reveille Gap road. And nobody gets into that back country unless LeBard or Siebold wants 'em to. I bet a good look in there would show some J P Connected stuff."

"From what Pinderlee told me, LeBard runs a Sixty-six iron and Siebold a Long S," Hanford said. "You couldn't possibly blot a J P Connected brand into either of them."

"Maybe," said Tap sententiously, "they didn't bother to blot."

"Go on," encouraged Hanford. "You're driving at something."

Tap slouched his weight into his off stirrup, reached for tobacco and spun up a smoke.

"Like this. The cattle Jess Pinderlee originally brought into this basin were breeding stock. You ever see a better breeding range than right here? Grass, water, good shelter. Pinderlee was no fool; he knew his country and what it was good for. Well, the strays he didn't have a chance to gather and so had to leave behind, were cows. And why should LeBard and Siebold — and maybe others — worry about how to blot a J P cow when they can slap their own iron on the calf that cow drops?"

Hanford, reaching for Tap's tobacco, murmured drily.

"Where'd you learn to be so darn smart?"

Tap grinned, straightened and pointed again, this time to the northeast.

"Get that flash of sun on window glass, way yonder? That's Long S, Buck Siebold's headquarters. You can't see LeBard's Sixty-six layout from here; it's hid down behind a ridge. You want to ride in there?"

Hanford considered while he built and lit his cigarette. Then he nodded briefly.

"Why not? We got all day."

Some time later they struck into a dim trace which worked an irregular, twisting way east and west. When they had crossed it, Tap said:

"Another old military road. Generally accepted as the north limit of the Reservation range. We're on somebody else's land now."

The road divided the character of the country as definitely as it marked limit of ownership. Where there had been low and easy sloped timber ridges, here now were crests and rims which pitched steeply up, and what had been relatively broad and generous meadows became narrowing gulches. Some grass clung to the sides of these, and here and there a pocket or pothole showed to offer a little greater extent of graze. But for the most part, this was browsing, rather than grazing range.

"If this is the best they got, I can see why LeBard and Siebold don't want to give up Reservation grass," Hanford said.

"Don't let this stretch fool you," Tap cautioned. "It's the poorest range in the basin. Further back there's a scatter of little valleys that produce some mighty fat cattle for LeBard and Siebold."

They moved deeper into the broken country and climbed the run of a gulch which funneled upward between two sugar loaf crests. Beyond these the country leveled somewhat, and here, abruptly, Tap swung his horse behind a clump of buckbrush and gave terse warning.

"Watch it!"

Hanford put the roan behind the same thicket and from this shelter watched three riders move at a fast jog across a clearing, some ninety or a hundred yards out. Leading, was Frenchy LeBard. The others Hanford had never seen before. They were heading east and were soon gone, dipping from view past the point of a run.

Tap Timberlake let out a slow breath of relief.

"Close! Had we busted right out in front of them, there might have been the makings of a mean ruckus. That Frenchy LeBard, he's a rattlesnake. You never know whether he'll just stay coiled, or whether he'll strike."

"Any time he wants it so, he can have it," Hanford said harshly. "I'm not forgetting Reed Challis. I never will. There's a strange thing. I'd known the man hardly a day, yet somehow I liked him — plenty! So, if my luck holds, LeBard answers to me for that!"

"Not at a hundred yards," Tap said soberly. "Not with him carrying a rifle on his saddle and you with only a belt gun. I don't know how good you are with that Colt.

Maybe awful good. But no man is good enough to have any chance with a belt gun against a rifle at a distance. I ain't trying to tell you your business, but were I you, I'd think about slinging a rifle to my saddle. It could easy be the difference between living or dying."

"Something I'll have to attend to, all right," Hanford admitted. "Wonder where those three would be going?"

"Siebold's mebbe. More likely to Crown. One was Speck Mastick. He's a Crown hand. With King Morgan's meeting busted up the way it was last night, mebbe he's figuring to hold another at Crown headquarters, and sent Mastick after LeBard."

"Makes sense," said Hanford. "Well, with LeBard out of the way, now's a good chance to look around. Who was the third one?"

Tap shook his head. "Don't know his name. He's fairly recent in the basin, I think. I've seen him with LeBard a couple of times. Didn't strike me as being exactly full of sweetness and light. LeBard has one other rider. A big, hulking jigger with a pea-sized brain. Strong as a horse and works like one."

They fell into the trail LeBard and the other two were on and went the other way along it. It took them across a leveling benchland, worked through a stand of scrub timber, then pitched down toward a little valley beyond. Here they met with a drift of wood smoke.

Out on the valley flat in a small pole corral, some dozen or fifteen white-faced cows were grouped, along with an equal number of calves. A saddle mount stood by the corral fence, drowsing in the morning sun. A short way apart a burly hulk of a man squatted on his heels and fed wood into a fire.

"Speak of the devil!" Tap murmured. "Coony Ells. Looks like he might be working up a branding fire. Which sets me to wondering."

"Wondering — what?"

"Like this. Jess Pinderlee brought only straight white face stock into the basin, and all those cows down there are white faces. But Frenchy LeBard, most of his herd is mixed stuff. So, I'm wondering what brands those cows are carrying?"

"Did I say you were smart?" Hanford drawled. "Let's go find out."

Tap carried a scabbarded Winchester under his stirrup leather. Now he slid this free and carried it in his right hand, butt resting against his hip, barrel angled upward so that it was easily visible.

"We'll drive straight in. Like I said, Coony ain't exactly bright in the head, and when he sees this Winchester all ready to go, likely he'll gentle right down."

They left the slope at a run and were within a hundred and fifty yards of the man by the fire before he lunged erect, turned and stared. They had cut this distance another fifty before the lumbering, slow-witted fellow was able to wring any significance out of their abrupt appearance. Then he turned, took a step or two toward his horse, but stopped as Tap's call sailed forward.

"Stay put, Coony! Won't be a lick of trouble if you stay put!"

Coony Ells stayed as he was, staring sullenly. But as Hanford and Tap swung to a stop beside the fire, he had his heavy say.

"What the hell's the idea, chargin' in on a man this way? Wavin' a gun and everything. Yeah, what's the idea?"

"Just a little something we want to check on," Tap told him. "Reason I had a gun ready was so you wouldn't go getting ideas you shouldn't and mebbe get hurt. Aiming to do a chore of branding, Coony?"

Coony Ells nodded heavily. "Yeah — brandin'. What's it to you?"

"Why," grinned Tap, "we're just interested in seeing which brands you aim to put on what, that's all."

Clay Hanford had reined over close to the corral and had his look. He turned to Tap, nodding.

"You called it. This is all J P Connected stuff."

He rode over to Coony Ells's horse. Coony had taken off his belt and gun and hung these on his saddle horn for greater freedom in his branding chore. Also, slung to Coony's saddle in a worn, scorched buckskin sheath, was a running iron.

Hanford unloaded the gun and carried the running iron with him as he rode back to the fire. There was a stamp iron pushed into flames. Hanford nodded toward it.

"Have a look, Tap. See what it reads."

"From here," Tap said, as he swung down, "I'd bet heavy that it's a Sixty-six." He pulled the stamp iron from the fire, glanced at the heating end of it. "And I'd win my bet."

Hanford, straightening in his saddle, stared down into Coony's dull, surly eyes.

"Friend," he said, "maybe you didn't know it, but I happen to own the cows in that corral. And, seeing that the calves obviously belong to the cows, I own them, too.

Now you wouldn't be set to heat that stamp iron unless you were going to use it. On the calves, maybe?"

Coony Ells shifted ponderously from one foot to the other and his glance slid away.

"I only do what the boss tells me to do," he blurted.

"And this running iron," went on Hanford. "I suppose when you meet up with a stray J P cow with a calf anywhere, right then and there you make it a Sixty-six calf?"

Coony made another attempt to meet Hanford's frosty, boring regard, but couldn't. He licked his lips.

"I do what I'm told, that's all."

"Fine!" said Hanford crisply. "For a little while you're going to do just as I tell you. First, we saw LeBard and two others heading out up above. Where were they going?"

"Crown," mumbled Coony. "Old man Morgan's callin' another meetin'."

Hanford swung his head. "Which means they'll be gone about how long, Tap?"

Tap computed silently, eyes pinched down in thought. Then he tipped a shoulder.

"Depends on how long Morgan holds 'em, of course. The meetin' should last until noon, easy. Then they'll eat. I'd say it would be a pretty sound gamble that LeBard won't be showing back here before well along in the afternoon. And should he decide to swing by town, then it could be after dark. And," Tap added, eagerly guessing what was in Hanford's mind, "we can easy have those calves made into honest Rafter H critters long before that."

"And the cows?"

"Cows, too, if we had a big strong feller like Coony to help."

"Coony," said Hanford, "is going to help!"

He put his glance on Coony Ells again. At what he saw in Hanford's eyes, Coony backed up a clumsy step, stuttering.

"Me help what — how — ?"

"This is the way it is," Hanford told him bleakly. "Men have been hung and men have been shot for putting their brand on the calves of another man's cows. Saying you were only doing what LeBard told you to do doesn't necessarily excuse you. Tap and me, we could string you up to the handiest tree right now, and honest men everywhere would say you had it coming. I'm offering you a break. You help — you really help us brand the calves and vent the J P iron on the cows to my Rafter H, and you ride off scot free. Otherwise — !" He began unstrapping the rawhide riata from his saddle.

Coony Ells hesitated, and Tap Timberlake spoke.

"Better listen, Coony. Better listen good. This ain't no make-believe."

Coony licked his heavy, out-rolling lips again. In the relatively stagnant processes of his mind, he weighed the odds and the penalty. He was afraid of Frenchy LeBard. He was more afraid just now of Clay Hanford, of this lean, cold jawed man with the frosty gray eyes. For LeBard wasn't present and Hanford was. The way Coony's mind worked, that decided it. He fell back on his favorite excuse.

"I do what I'm ordered to do. Long as I got to help, I'll help."

And he did, prodigiously.

For Coony Ells owned one thing of which he was inordinately, almost childishly proud. His strength, his slow, tremendous, bull strength. It was the one possession which set him up with other men, or above them. Others might be faster in the head, faster with a gun, faster afoot and in general physical movement. But when it came to straight brute power, none could match him. Coony knew this and he never missed an opportunity to let others know it. Like now.

He would rope a calf and when Tap opened the corral gate enough to let the bucking, bawling little animal through, haul it to him, hand over hand, with no more apparent effort than an average man would with a small terrier dog. Then, with one big, effortless heave, he would flip and hold it while Hanford, tending fire and wielding the running iron, set a Rafter H high on the near hip, then with pocket knife swallow-forked both ears. After which the calf was released and Coony would go after another one.

They worked fast and when done with the calves started right in on the cows. Here was a far sterner chore, with Tap and Coony maneuvering mostly from their saddles. Big and ponderous as he was, Coony Ells knew how to handle a rope, while his horse was a particularly good one at this sort of thing.

Cows were roped, thrown and stretched, and Hanford moved fast with the running iron. Jess Pinderlee's ear mark was swallowfork right and left, which Hanford had known when he registered his own, so now there was no need of change on these cows.

Critters bawled. Smoke winnowed. Sweat ran copiously. Hanford used his jumper to grip the hot running iron. Even so he picked up several scorches. Coony, leaving his saddle to help handle a particularly obstreperous critter, got in the way of a flailing hoove, and thereafter limped. Yet still did his full share and more.

It was done, finally. Clay Hanford straightened and stretched and with honest admiration looked at Coony Ells through sweat filled eyes.

"In your way, big fellow, you're a lot of man. You ever want to get on the honest side of this argument, look me up. Hanford is the name. I own the Reservation range."

"Heard about you at breakfast this morning," Coony said. "You won't last. Pinderlee didn't. You won't either."

"I'll last," Hanford said flatly. "And remember — I asked you." He turned to Tap. "Let's get going. We got a drive ahead of us."

Tap nodded. "I figured it so. Now this is the kind of day I really like. Coony, you better come along. LeBard's going to be awful damn mad over this."

Coony did not answer, just tramped to his horse, swung up and headed for the far end of the little valley, gathering in and coiling his riata as he rode. By the time Hanford and Tap had the cows and calves bunched and on the move, Coony Ells was out of sight.

★ ★ ★

From a stretch of level ground at the crest of a low slope, Crown headquarters looked west across the full sweep of Fandango Basin. In back of it the country ran away to meet the southern swing of the Greystone Hills. Out of these hills tumbled the southern fork of May Day Creek, making a swing that brought it close behind headquarters, thence angling away to join North Fork, some five miles further on.

The headquarters stood in the form of a square. There were some who had cynically remarked on this fort-like arrangement, branding it as just one more indication of King Morgan's range pirate complex. Right or wrong, the arrangement was efficient.

Facing the basin, the ranchhouse stretched long and low and porched its full length, to fill the west end of the square. The bunkhouse, cookhouse and several store rooms made up the south side. North side was saddle and harness shed, blacksmith shop and shelters for a buckboard, a spring wagon, and a heavy Merivale work wagon. East were the barns and feed sheds. Beyond these, the corrals. In the approximate center of the square thus formed a big pine tree towered, fenced about with a hitching rail.

King Morgan had his office at the south end of the ranchhouse. Next to this was a room in which he slept, and another holding beds for Price and Lute. Lute regularly slept here, but Price only occasionally, preferring as a rule, the bunkhouse with the crew. The central part of the house was made up of a big living room and an equally spacious kitchen, which opened in the rear. The north end of the house was Lear Morgan's quarters.

This morning, Price Morgan awoke in his bed in the ranchhouse for a change. Arrogantly proud, and in the bitter depths because of the manner in which Clay Hanford had beaten him down, on reaching home last night Price had no heart to listen to any comment, or answer any questions concerning the affair. So he had avoided the bunkhouse.

Price Morgan had whipped his share of men, and had known a dark pride in his ability to do this. But last night he had lain on the floor of the Ute House barroom, beaten senseless by the fists of Clay Hanford, and he writhed before the bitter truth of it. He had heard his father arise in the next room, and his brother Lute in this one, and had lain with eyes closed, waiting for them to leave the house. For he knew he could expect sarcastic remarks from Lute and some condemnation from his father.

The fragrance of hot coffee reached him and brought him out of his blankets finally. As he dressed he was surprised at how sore and stiff he was, all over. If you were hit hard enough, he reflected darkly, evidently the results were not limited merely to the spot where the blow landed, but spread all through you.

He went out into the kitchen and found Lear there. In simple gingham, and with her hair hanging in a heavy braid between her shoulders, she looked very young and girlish. Price had never been very close to this sister of his, never particularly kind, or unkind, for that matter. To him she just was, that was all, and he had pretty much taken her for granted. His own preference for company was the wilder, rougher atmosphere of the crew and the harsh authority of his father, a thing which seemed somehow to pass on to him a degree of strength.

He had a wash, finding his bruised lips puffed and tender. There was another bruise on the side of his neck, close up under his ear. When he pulled a chair up to the table, Lear set his breakfast before him. She sat down across from him, sipping a cup of coffee. She waited until he had taken the first edge off his hunger, then spoke quietly.

"Price, what's to become of us?"

He started, jerked his head up and stared. And thought he had never seen this degree of soberness and thoughtful questioning in his sister's eyes before.

"Don't know what you're driving at," he blurted. "What do you mean?"

"Exactly what I said. What's to become of us with — with everybody hating us?" Lear's voice broke just a trifle.

Price stared again. "Everybody hating us! How do you know they do?"

"I know," Lear said. "I can tell by the way they look at us. Oh, some may act friendly, but that's because they fear us. Underneath, they really hate us."

Price shook his head, as in bemused wonder. "You fool girl — you've been having nightmares."

"I've been thinking," Lear retorted. "For the first time in my life, I guess, I've been really thinking. And — I'm afraid!"

"Afraid!" Price scoffed. "What have you got to be afraid of? Sure, there's some who hate us. When you're the head of the pack there's always some who'll hate you. Who gives a damn about that? We're Morgans, ain't we? And what we say in this basin, goes!"

"Like — like Marshal Challis being killed, last night? Did we have anything to say about — that?"

Price came up still straighter in his chair. "Where did you hear about it?"

"I was awake when Dad and the rest of you came in from town last night. I overheard some remarks. This morning I asked Lute about it, straight out."

"Well, it happened," Price acknowledged. "But it was between Challis and Frenchy LeBard. Nothing for you to get concerned over."

"But I am concerned!" Lear flared. "I'm concerned because Marshal Challis was a good man, a — a nice man, courteous and polite whenever I met him. Always there was the slightest bow, always he tipped his hat. Maybe — maybe that means nothing to you, but it meant something to me. It made me feel fine and good, like I was really a lady. Like he was doing it, not because I happened to be Lear Morgan, but because I was that real lady."

Lear choked a little, brushed a hand across her eyes and went on, a thread of fierce spirit in her words.

"That Frenchy LeBard — that crude, treacherous animal! He never tipped his hat to a lady in his life. And he cold-bloodedly shot Marshal Challis in the back. Lute said he did!"

Price swung his shoulders irritably. "There's times when Lute talks too damn much!"

Lear brushed her hand across her eyes again, then asked, in a more subdued tone:

"You fought last night, too, didn't you? I see bruises."

Slow crimson crept through Price's cheeks. "Didn't amount to much," he said gruffly. "Forget it — forget all of it! Such things are the affairs of men. All you have to do is just remember that you're a Morgan. And act like one."

Lear sat quietly for a time, sipping her coffee, studying her brother across the rim of her cup. When he finished eating and sat back for a moment, reaching for his smoking, she asked another question.

"Price, am I being waved in front of Buck Siebold?"

"Waved in front of Buck Siebold!" exclaimed Price. "For God's sake — where'd you get that idea? Who put that nonsense in your head?"

"Never mind where or who," Lear said evenly. "I asked a fair question and I'd like a fair answer. Am I being waved in front of Buck Siebold?"

Deepening irritation gripped Price. Working at building a cigarette he tore a paper, spilled tobacco, swore, then began afresh, spinning up a smoke. Not until he had this safely lipped and alight and had pushed to his feet, did he answer.

"Buck's a good feller. Yeah, he's all right. And a friend of ours. Naturally it don't hurt for you to treat our friends nice."

"Oh, naturally," said Lear tonelessly. She got up and began clearing away the dishes.

Leaving, Price paused in the doorway and looked back at her. It struck him that she was suddenly clothed in a sort of forlorn loneliness, and he sought guiltily for something to say that might improve the moment. But no proper words came and he turned and went out.

Lear moved on with her household tasks. She washed up the breakfast dishes, then made her bed and tidied up her room. After which she went to the other end of the house to make the beds and clean up in her father's room and that of her brothers. She was done with this and back in the kitchen when she picked up the mutter of hoofs and she looked out to see Buck Siebold ride in past the blacksmith shop and pull up at the hitch rail under the pine tree. He did not dismount immediately but sat looking across at the kitchen door and window. Hoping, Lear knew, for a glimpse of her.

King Morgan emerged from the bunk-house and walked over to Siebold, who now stepped down. Under his pushed back hat this man had hair like so much cotton tow. He had little ears, pinned flat against his skull, and his neck ran up, wide and thick. There was about him no lightness, no ease or grace of movement. He was stocky and burly and coarse of feature, with down sloped shoulders and long, simian arms. When he gave grinning answer to something King Morgan said, his heavy lips fell away from big, square teeth.

Lear remembered what Tap Timberlake had called Buck Siebold. A gorilla, a human gorilla. That was what Tap had called him. Lear shivered and hurried from the kitchen to her own room and quarters. Here, from another window, she could look far out over all of Fandango Basin, now glowing under the morning sun.

Out there somewhere was Tap Timberlake. Tap — the cheerful, depend-able one, staunch companion of an earlier day. She remembered what he had said about the good times they had once had to-gether, he and she. And the remark he'd made of how she used to laugh, like some happy little kid. . . .

Abruptly there was a lump in Lear Morgan's throat, and tears in her eyes, and the words she spoke were soft and choked.

"Oh — Tap — Tap! I want to laugh again — like that — !"

SEVEN

Rusty Acuff rode in at Crown only a few minutes after Buck Siebold, but it was a good hour later before Frenchy LeBard arrived, along with Speck Mastick and his own Sixty-six rider, one Harry Adan. Impatient in this thing, King Morgan immediately waved LeBard over to his office, where Siebold and Acuff waited, along with Price and Lute Morgan, and Cob Jacklyn, Crown's foreman.

King Morgan wasted no time getting down to business. He took the chair at the table which served him as a desk, and drifted a harsh, frowning glance around at the others. He showed the effects of a night of not too much sleep, and a great deal of glowering introspection. His blocky face showed strong color and his eyes held the congested look that told of banked anger: The harshness that was in his eyes, rang in his voice.

"I called this gather because the way things went in town last night, we didn't settle everything that needs settling. Also, there's a new angle to be considered. We'll get around to that, later. First, about this fellow, Hanford, and what we're going to do with him. I want some opinions on that."

"The way you felt last night, King, is still good enough for me," Buck Siebold said heavily. "He had a lot of luck, last night — he got out of town with a whole skin. We can see to it that he doesn't have the same kind of luck, next time."

Frenchy LeBard nodded, eyes moiling. Rusty Acuff said nothing, which was his usual way. But there was a pull of expression in his scarred face and about his eyes which reflected some degree of troubled doubt. However, in the past his silence had always meant assent, and now King Morgan so judged it.

Difference of opinion came, however, and from a source little suspected.

"I can't go along with that sort of thing, Mr. Morgan," said Cob Jacklyn quietly.

It startled them, because this was the first time any of them had ever heard this leathery, laconic, still faced man disagree openly in opinion with his boss. Most startled of all was King Morgan himself. Autocratic to the point of utter domination, he had seldom tolerated or accepted opinion other than his own, particularly if the matter be one of real consequence. Yet here was his own foreman in flat disagreement with him. Sheer astonishment held him silent for the moment, which Cob Jacklyn seized upon to enlarge his statement.

"That sort of thing was never any good, and I can't go along with it!"

Frenchy LeBard broke the following pause, sneering.

"Turning soft, Jacklyn?"

Cob Jacklyn was a sparely built man, with the flat, tight flanks of one who had spent much of his life in a saddle. His cheeks were weathered to the consistency of leather and he could have been anywhere from forty to fifty years of age. He knew cattle thoroughly, and he handled men with a brief, sure authority, an authority backed up by a pair of gray-green eyes that carried an impact difficult to face. He put that impact on LeBard now, and his words rang with a contempt beyond limit.

"Don't speak to me, you damned dog! Of course you're for killing, just like you killed last night. When you didn't have the nerve to face up to a brave man when he called you, but crawled out with your tail between your legs, then hid in the dark to shoot him in the back. That was murder, dirty, cowardly, cold-blooded murder. It's my regret, LeBard, that whoever it was tried to dust you, didn't get you instead of your horse. Here is my last word to you. If I ever catch you sneaking around my back trail, I'll gun you down like I would any other rabid animal!"

Listening, the astonishment in King Morgan became swift anger.

"Jacklyn," he rapped, "what in hell's the matter with you? You gone crazy? That's no way to talk to Frenchy."

Cob Jacklyn looked at King Morgan and his reply ran steady.

"It's my way, Mr. Morgan. An open, honest showdown is one thing. Shoot-in-the-back murder is something else again. And I want no part of it, or do I want to have anything to do with the kind of sneaking whelp who goes in for that sort of thing!"

"You didn't say anything like this last night," charged Morgan.

"I didn't have a chance to say anything last night; too many other things were happening. Else I'd have had my say, all right. Any way, I'm having it now."

King Morgan stared at him, anger deepening.

"Wouldn't be trying to stretch your authority, by any chance?"

"No," Cob Jacklyn said, even and quiet. "Nothing like that. Just having my say, which I'm not done with. When I am, I'll let you decide something, Mr. Morgan. First, I'll have no part in the planned murder of a good man. Second, what Hack Williamson said last night was the exact truth. Reservation grass is no longer free grass. It ceased being so the moment Jess Pinderlee bought it. Your big mistake, Mr. Morgan, was that you didn't buy it yourself. You knew the government had it up for sale. So did the rest of you."

His glance touched the others briefly.

"Yes, you all knew it could be bought. But maybe all of you were just a little bit greedy. You'd been grazing that grass free for so long, you just couldn't bring yourselves to the idea of paying for it. You figured you could hang on to it by other means, such as closing the basin to outsiders. It was an idea that didn't work. Pinderlee bought the Reservation range and moved in."

"What of it?" blurted Buck Siebold, heavily sarcastic. "He ain't here now, is he? We ran him out."

"That's right," agreed Jacklyn, nodding. "We ran him out. At which I helped. Because Pinderlee was not a lone man, fighting for his rights, but because he was a big owner with a crusty crew. And because Pinderlee has tromped down many a weaker man, getting where he is. So — I helped run him out. But I won't do the same with this Clay Hanford."

"Why?" probed Siebold. "You never saw the man in your life before last night. Why you backing away from him?"

"Perhaps for several reasons you wouldn't understand, Buck," Jacklyn said, returning the sarcasm. "I'll give you one. Because he represents that inevitability Hack Williamson spoke of. I knew when we ran Pinderlee out, that it wouldn't last. Either he'd come back, bigger and stronger than ever, or somebody else would show in his place. Somebody did. Clay Hanford. Now you're set to either kill him or run him out. My feeling is that in that little deal you could be faced with a damn tough chore. And even should you put it over, it's only a matter of time before you'll have to face the same setup against another man or another outfit."

"All right," said King Morgan savagely, "then we'll face them. We'll give them the same medicine. We'll go on that way. We'll go on — !"

"Just so," Cob Jacklyn cut in. "You'll go on fighting the inevitable, all the time moving closer to the day when you'll destroy yourself, along with Crown and all that it could stand for. Best think of it, Mr. Morgan. There's still time to admit the facts and face them."

King Morgan stared at him as if unable to understand.

"The only fact I see is that either you've lost your mind, or like Frenchy said, you're turning soft. Best thing you can do is get out of here and attend to ranch affairs with the rest of the crew. I'll handle this matter in my own way."

Cob Jacklyn met and held Morgan's congested gaze. Then, as though the gesture expressed some regret, shook his head slightly.

"I said I'd let you decide something for me, Mr. Morgan. You just did." He walked to the door, paused and had another look around the room. "One other thing. When you get all through hating Clay Hanford, you'll probably start hating Hack Williamson. Let it stop there. Hate him if you want, and be damned to you. But harm him or his in any way and you'll answer to me. Then you'll find out if I'm soft or not! Mr. Morgan, you can leave my time with Pete Garth at the Golden, next time you're in town."

Saying which, Cob Jacklyn walked out,

spare and straight and decisive.

Long had Cob Jacklyn ridden at the right hand of King Morgan, until it seemed he was as much a part of the ranch as was Morgan himself. That he would be quitting Crown now, did not seem reasonable. King Morgan flatly refused to believe it. He turned to Price.

"Go get that touchy damn fool back in here. I'll smooth his feathers. Rest of you keep your remarks to yourself."

Price went out.

King Morgan dug a cigar from his vest pocket, lit it and puffed heavily, staring at the door through the smoke. Shortly Price returned. He looked at his father and shook his head.

"He's not coming back."

King Morgan surged erect. "I'll see about that!"

He tramped out and along to the bunkhouse. Here Cob Jacklyn stood alone by his bunk, sorting some odds and ends into his warbag. Morgan struck the flat of his hand against the door post.

"Enough of this nonsense, Cob. Come on back to the office."

Jacklyn straightened and faced him impassively. "I thought I'd made it clear, Mr. Morgan. I'm riding out. I'm quitting Crown."

"For God's sake — why? Over a little raw-hiding — a squabble of words?"

"No. Not over that, though it helped me make up my mind. Mainly I'm quitting because Crown is heading straight into something I just can't swallow. I'll fight for my outfit so long as there's at least some semblance of right at stake. But damned if I'll be any part of out and out piracy, or of a pack set to hunt down and destroy a man merely because he's standing up for his lawful rights!"

"Lawful rights!" Morgan exploded. "You call it lawful for this fellow Hanford to claim Reservation range at the price of a single dollar? You call a deal like that, legal?"

"I do," Jacklyn said steadily. "From what I saw of Hanford last night I'm sure of a couple of things. One is that he's not bluffing. The other is that he's no fool. And only a fool would try a bluff in an affair like this. I don't care if Hanford bought the range for a dollar or a dime. It's his, and his stand is legal."

King Morgan swung a violent, disagreeing hand.

"Not with me, it isn't! There's no room for that fellow in Fandango Basin — no room at all. Now quit being so damned proud about it. Come on back to the office and we'll figure out how we're going to handle him."

Again Cob Jacklyn looked King Morgan over carefully and again he shook his head, with that same glimmer of regret, as if saying goodbye to something.

"There was a time, Mr. Morgan, when it was a matter of pride with me, riding for Crown. For while we can't all own a big cattle outfit, even as a hired hand a man can know a pride in it as deep, almost, as that of the owner. Which is a fine thing, Mr. Morgan. For it can give a man like me real purpose in life. And as long as a man rides for his outfit with honest pride, then he also rides with self-respect. But if he rides for an outfit when he no longer does so with pride, then he has lost his self-respect. And I aim to keep mine."

Cob Jacklyn closed his warbag, picked it up along with a pair of well-worn saddle-bags, then reached down a Winchester rifle from the wall pegs above his bunk. Burdened with these things he moved to the door, there to face King Morgan at short range. The ghost of a sardonic smile twisted his lips.

"How long have I ridden for Crown, Mr. Morgan? Better than twenty years? Quite a chunk out of a man's life. And what have I

156

got to show for it? What you see me with, here, and a horse and saddle, out at the corrals. Well, about that I'm not kicking. A saddle hand seldom owns anything more. Yet, for these things I gave you twenty years of my life. What do you offer in return? Just the opinion that I've turned soft, because I insist on hanging on to some shreds of decency and self-respect. And in a showdown of differences, you take sides with a dirty, murdering whelp — that Frenchy LeBard. Mr. Morgan, you're just not good enough man for me to ride with any longer!"

By the time Cob Jacklyn finished, all trace of the sardonic smile was gone. In its place his mouth was tight drawn and a hurt bitterness blazed in his eyes. He pushed past King Morgan and moved across the compound toward the corrals.

King Morgan watched him, expressions of anger, uncertainty, hesitation, then anger again, one after another, sweeping across his face. Finally he cursed, turned, and tramped back to the office.

In her kitchen again and from its windows trying to keep restless and worried account of what was going on about headquarters, Lear Morgan had observed this by-play between her father and Cob Jacklyn at the bunkhouse door. She saw Jacklyn head for the corrals with his load of gear, and correctly read the significance of it. She had seen riders heading the same way, burdened the same way before, and it always meant but one thing. They were done with Crown!

Which, in general, meant nothing in particular to her, one way or the other. For riders were always hiring on, staying for a while, then leaving again: they were, for the most part, a restless, footloose breed. But to see Cob Jacklyn leaving — that was different! Why, as far back as she could remember, Cob Jacklyn had been part of Crown. Her father's right hand man. Cob Jacklyn, foreman. The man who ran the crew.

Many times in the past, Cob Jacklyn had sat in this very kitchen, eating breakfast with her father while they talked over ranch affairs and the business of the day ahead. Lear had always liked him. He was a neat man, clean shaven, careful of his manners, quiet and polite in her presence. And in some ways was more kindly and understanding than her own masculine kin.

Now, plainly, he was leaving, and Lear's uneasiness and worry deepened. What, she wondered, had happened and was happening to bring this thing about? The question was parent to the answering action. She went quietly into the south wing of the ranchhouse, into her father's room, an inner wall of which was in common with the office. She stood close to this wall and listened.

In the office, with King Morgan's return, there was a period of uneasy, questioning silence. The cattleman had resumed his chair at the table, and he sat there for a little time, staring at nothing with bleak, hooded eyes. Harshly he cleared his throat.

"Cob Jacklyn is no longer a part of Crown," he announced. "Not being with us, he could very well be against us. We will watch out for that. Now back to our original business. This fellow Hanford. It's agreed we go after him? Good enough. Now for ways and means."

Frenchy LeBard spoke. "He won't be alone. He had help last night. The shots that downed my horse came from up past Gorman's store. And that wasn't where Hanford was."

"Who could it have been?"

"Nobody he brought in with him." Lute Morgan spoke for the first time. "He came into the basin alone, and there were no strangers showing either before or after him. Maybe we better face something. Which is that not everybody in Fandango Basin is fond of us. There are some who would jump at the chance to tie in with anybody who's against us."

"You mean maybe, Running W — Williamson's outfit?" asked Buck Siebold.

"No!" said Lute sharply. "I don't mean Running W. Let's keep Running W out of this. Hack Williamson was neutral against Pinderlee, and he stands to be neutral in this. We'll leave him so!"

"Maybe we will," King Morgan growled. "I'm considerable out of patience with Hack Williamson. I've seen Running W cows on Reservation grass, so damned if I can see his claim to acting so hoity-toity and noble. Yeah — maybe we'll leave him to his damned neutrality — and maybe we won't. It'll depend on several things. And you —" here he put his glance on Lute, "you'll go along with whatever decision the rest of us come to. Frenchy, you were the one shot at. You got any ideas?"

LeBard shrugged. "Might try a guess."

"All right, make it."

"Tap Timberlake, maybe. And Frank Billings. They're about the only really foot-loose ones in the basin. And with everything to gain and damn little to lose, should they side in with Hanford."

King Morgan considered a moment, then

nodded. "Makes sense. And if true, they'll get the same treatment as Hanford. They'll get no mercy from me!"

The talk went on, though somewhat haltingly. The walkout of Cob Jacklyn was a jarring, unsettling note they could not immediately put aside. It had thrown a knife of uncertainty into things, and, though declarations of purpose were made, these did not as yet carry a tone of complete conviction. All of which King Morgan sensed and fumed against. He was glad when the triangle at the cook shack beat out its noontime summons across the compound.

"We'll eat," he announced, getting to his feet. "Afterwards, we'll talk out something definite."

Shortly after King Morgan and the others went into the cookshack, Lear Morgan emerged from the ranch house kitchen and moved quickly through the compound to the feed shed and corral area. She had done a fast job of putting up her hair, and had changed from household gingham to divided skirt and blouse and riding boots.

Range bred and raised, she caught and saddled with an ease and swiftness to match any man. She rode straight south from the corrals along a trail which presently turned west toward the Reveille Gap road, meeting

161

up with this some two miles below Crown headquarters. On the trail she had traveled at a fast jog, but now, with the road opening before her, she lifted her pony to a reaching lope, anxious for town.

Coming into Morgan Junction, her glance searched the street and identified the saddle mount in front of the Ute House. She put her own pony up to the rail and hurried into the hotel. Mike Scorry, passing through the narrow lobby, stopped and surveyed her gravely, round face expressionless.

"Cob Jacklyn," Lear asked, "have you seen him, Mr. Scorry?"

The hotel owner nodded, inclining his head toward the dining room. In here, Cob Jacklyn sat at a table at the far end of the room. Lear went along and stopped beside him.

"Cob — I want to talk to you."

He came to his feet, faced her levelly. "Certainly, Lear. But don't try and change my mind. It won't do any good. I'm through at Crown."

"It — it isn't that, Cob — though I truly feel very badly about it. This — is something else."

He nodded. "Sit down."

She took the chair across from him, stripping off her buckskin gloves.

162

"I'd enjoy buying your dinner," he said. "I'll call the cook —"

She shook her head quickly. "I don't want anything. But you go ahead with yours."

He did so, while he waited and wondered. Down across the years he had watched Lear Morgan grow up in that most difficult of surroundings for a girl, in a household peopled entirely by men. That she had emerged at all reasonably balanced, was tribute to a basic and enduring character fiber.

Inevitably, with it ever present and all around her, she had taken on a degree of the Morgan insolence and arrogance, yet Cob Jacklyn had always felt that in her this was more of an unconscious pose than anything else, an artificial shield to hide shyness and uncertainty.

But there was nothing arrogant about her now, nothing insolent. Instead, a strained and solemn-eyed soberness.

"Cob," she said, "would you have any idea where you might find Tap Timberlake?"

He looked at her in some wonderment. "Tap Timberlake? Afraid I can't name any exact spot, off hand. But by prowling a bit I think I might locate him. Why?"

"Will you find him, as — as a favor to me?" She leaned forward in her intensity of feeling.

"And if I do, then what?"

"Tell him not to ride with this stranger — this Clay Hanford. Not to work with him against Crown."

A gleam came into Jacklyn's eyes. "Suppose you tell me the rest of it."

She did so, in little, hesitating, gusty outbursts. She told how, by standing close to the common wall between the ranch office and her father's room, she had managed to pick up some of the talk that went on in the office.

"I'm afraid, Cob," she ended. "Of a sudden I've the feeling that I don't know my father any more, that I haven't known him for a long time, that he is virtually a stranger to me. I don't understand him, or how he thinks. Price and Lute, they're almost as bad, and they'll do what father tells them to do. Lute might barely argue some, but Price will follow blindly. Those other men, the ones father calls his friends — Buck Siebold, Frenchy LeBard, Rusty Acuff — they give me the shivers, all of them. And they mean to hunt down Clay Hanford, hunt him down and kill him and any who ride with him!"

"You think Tap Timberlake may be riding with Hanford?"

"Almost sure of it. Father and the rest

think he is. And I heard father say that if Tap was riding with Hanford, he could expect no mercy. So I want you to find Tap and tell him that, Cob. Warn him to stay far away from Hanford."

Cob Jacklyn's studying glance was very steady. "Once," he said, "you and Tap were pretty good friends, weren't you?"

Lear nodded quickly, a tide of color washing up her throat and across her face.

"And still would like to be?"

She nodded again, a glimmer of moisture in her eyes.

"I'll take a ride, Lear." Jacklyn's tone turned gentle. "I'll find Tap and tell him what you said. I'll give him your warning. But I'm afraid it won't do any good, not if I know human nature. If Tap has joined up with Hanford, he won't leave him. For he's been long waiting, I think, for someone like Hanford to show up. Tap is no coward, Lear. He won't run, and he's not the sort to let down a man who trusts him. But I'll tell him what you said."

Lear blinked, brushed a hand across her eyes.

"Thanks, Cob — thanks. You always were — good to me."

She got up and went out and Cob's glance followed her, grave and regretful. He went after the rest of his food a trifle fiercely.

"King Morgan — you fool!" he murmured. "You arrogant, stubborn, crazy headed fool! Can't you see what you're throwing away — ?"

Back at Crown, noon meal done, King Morgan and the rest left the cookshack, stood for a little time in the compound, getting smokes going. And while they stood so, it was Coony Ells who came riding, a ponderous figure in the saddle. His horse was run out, dark with sweat, and with streaks of foam edging the saddle blanket. Frenchy LeBard, exclaiming, stepped out to meet him, gaunt and suspicious.

"What brings you here, Ells? What's wrong?"

Coony Ells told his story, brief and heavy and blurting. Frenchy LeBard cursed and came around to face King Morgan.

"You heard? Those cows and calves — Hanford took them right out of a corral of mine. Branded and earmarked the calves and vented the Pinderlee iron on the cows. And he had Timberlake helping him!"

"Hanford — he don't waste time, does he?" exclaimed Buck Siebold.

King Morgan waved an angry arm.

"We won't waste it, either. We're going after those fellows!"

EIGHT

It was full sundown when Clay Hanford and Tap Timberlake finally put their little gather of cows and calves into a meadow across the creek from the cabin headquarters. Getting the animals down out of the broken country of the Smokies and across the old military road which marked the north boundary of the Reservation range, they had driven steadily. Once on his own land, however, Hanford was content with a more leisurely pace.

A number of times they stopped to let the cows graze and the calves rest. Whenever this occurred, Tap circled back, watching the trail. But there had been no sign of anyone following. Along the last few miles both of them had carried one of the smaller, weaker calves across their saddles.

When Tap lifted his charge down to the meadow sod, he voiced his satisfaction.

"There y'are, you bald-faced little bummer. You're an honest-to-God Rafter H critter now, on your own range."

They crossed the creek to the corral. Woodsmoke was winnowing from the cabin chimney. Frank Billings showed and came over to them.

"You had me wondering some," he observed. "Didn't figure you to be gone this long."

"Didn't expect to be," Hanford admitted. Briefly he outlined what the day had held.

Billings showed his small, dry grin. "Now that's something! Critters of our own already, to keep an eye on. Shows we mean business. LeBard — he'll be fit to tie."

"I'm not done with Mister LeBard," Hanford said, significantly. "How was the day with you?"

"Had a visitor. Abe Kerwin, one of Hack Williamson's men. Brought word that Running W was going to get right at the chore of moving off any of their stuff that had drifted on to Reservation grass. Wanted us to know what they were about, when we see them riding Also, there's mebbe twenty-five or thirty head of J P Connected stuff hanging close in some alder brakes near the head of Lyle Canyon. Running W will help us dig them out, any time we're ready."

Listening in, Tap Timberlake nodded with emphasis.

"That's Hack Williamson for you. A

real square shooter."

If Hanford and Tap had been busy through the day, so had Frank Billings. Outside the cabin door was a wash bench holding water bucket and basin. Inside, two more bunks had been built, rust scoured from the stove and shelves added to the walls. Also, along with coffee, a pot of beans and another of go-to-hell stew simmered on the stove, and a pan of biscuits were brown and warm in the oven. Tap exclaimed boyishly.

"Lordy — lordy, let me at that grub! Been a long drag since breakfast."

They ate in silence until the first raw edge of hunger was blunted. Then Hanford made thoughtful comment.

"The fact that a Running W rider knew just where to find us, proves that our whereabouts is no mystery to anyone. And while the bunks Frank built look mighty comfortable, I think we'd be smart, now that we've made our first direct strike, to do our sleeping somewhere else for a day or two until we pick up the direction of the wind. We ever get trapped in this cabin, I wouldn't like our chances. We'd be fools not to recognize the odds. And until we cut them down or discourage them, our chances of staying healthy are better if we stay a couple of jumps ahead of the opposition with our thinking."

"Right as rain!" agreed Frank Billings emphatically. "At first King Morgan might have played with the idea that a lot of thunder bluster would scare us out. But when you picked those cows and calves right out of Frenchy LeBard's front yard, so to speak, it showed we mean business. So we can expect the gloves to come off, now."

Tap shrugged philosophically. "I've slept on the ground plenty of times before."

Hanford finished his meal, spun up a cigarette and got to his feet with a quick turn of decision.

"Where you going?" demanded Tap.

Hanford smiled faintly. "Following your sage advice. Heading for town after a saddle gun."

Tap stood up. "Another little ride won't hurt me."

Hanford waved him back. "You're staying here."

"But you might bump into something where I'll come in handy," Tap protested.

Hanford shook his head. "Won't be anything I can't handle."

Frank Billings began gathering up the dishes.

"Your bronc's been working all day.

Mine's loafed. Better take it."

"An idea," Hanford said. "I will."

The stars were high and their lustre silvering the night world by the time Clay Hanford rode in at Morgan Junction. Along the way he had mused over all that had taken place since he came into this far out, wild, basin country. Events that had piled up so fast. Even before he'd had chance to enter the basin proper, it seemed that the fates had been at work.

For there had been the night of the storm and the subsequent happenings at the Running W line camp on Piute Creek. There had been Moira Williamson, at first just a cry for help in the wild dark. Then, when he found her, she had been a full, living being in the circle of his arm and clinging to him while the wild creek waters surged hungrily about them.

Afterward, in the line camp cabin she was like a drenched, terrified child, weeping out her relief on his shoulder. But last night in town, in Joe Gorman's store, she had been a slim, poised young woman with lovely, deep-violet eyes that had, with their clarity and honesty, haunted him from the very first, and continued to.

Yet she wore Lute Morgan's ring, and he couldn't understand that. . . .

He did not enter town by the direct road, instead coming in from the timber to the west and making a careful survey of the street before crossing it to the dark end of Joe Gorman's hitch rail. From here he had another good look around before tramping quickly into the store. He was barely in time, for Gorman was preparing to close for the night.

"Won't keep you long," Hanford said. "I want a saddle gun and something to shoot in it."

Towering, bald-headed Joe Gorman eyed him without expression, nodded.

"Four on the rack. Three new ones and one that's been used. Take your choice. Used one's just as good as new. Feller traded it in against a saddle over a year ago. Scabbard goes with it. You can have it for what I allowed him. A buy at the price," Gorman named the sum.

"A buy if it's worth a damn," Hanford conceded. "Let's see it."

It was a Model '86 Winchester, caliber .38-56, the same as Tap Timberlake's rifle. Gorman had not misrepresented it. The weapon was in perfect condition.

"I'll take it," Hanford said. "And a couple of boxes of cartridges."

Gorman set out the ammunition and

made enigmatic remark.

"Some signs are bad — some good."

Hanford looked at him with narrowing eyes. "Now there's a right handed, left handed statement. I'm not sure I can straighten it out."

Gorman shrugged. "I could have been thinking out loud." He paused, then added, "I'm selling you a gun, ain't I?"

"That you are," Hanford admitted. "But is it because you want to, or because you figure you have to?"

"Mebbe it's like this," Gorman said, with slow emphasis. "Last night Moira Williamson told me how you pulled her out of Piute Creek. I happen to think a lot of that girl. Of Hack and Molly Williamson, too. I always have. And for a long time now I've been tired of taking orders." Tone and manner now became brisk. "You want something else, name it. Else, scatter along. It's time I closed up."

At the door, Hanford turned and looked back.

"Sorry I shook you up some yesterday morning."

Gorman waved an airy hand and for the first time the expressionless mask of his face loosened enough to let through a faint glint of humor.

"Think nothing of it. Maybe you did me a favor. You could have reminded me that I'm a man."

Out beside his horse, Clay Hanford broke open a box of cartridges, loaded the magazine of the rifle, then slung it in its boot under his near stirrup leather, butt to the rear. He stepped into his saddle and left town as he'd entered it. Behind him, the lights in Joe Gorman's store winked out.

Drawn back into the full dark of a timber clump, Cob Jacklyn watched a rider pass on the trail to town. Out there in the full open, star-glow spread a thin, silver sheen, and by this light Jacklyn identified the rider as Clay Hanford.

For some little time after Hanford passed, the ex-foreman of Crown held to the deep tree shadows, watching and listening. But presently, with night's silence unbroken by any sound or sign of following riders, he took the open trail and rode deeper into Reservation range.

He rode with an alert, reaching caution. It was this caution that had enabled him to pick up the first faint drum of approaching hoofs and thus swing off the trail to avoid Clay Hanford. And it was a caution which Jacklyn had decided a smart man should display at all times here in Fandango Basin, the way affairs were now breaking. Yes, indeed! A smart man would watch both sides of the trail as well as ahead and behind.

When he finally broke out into the clear of the creek meadows, there was no immediate sign of life in the old reservation ruins and surrounding cabins. He held his horse to a slow pacing across the meadow, his own wariness reaching and probing. The night was still, the air without movement. Hanging in it were faint odors of recently cooked food. Now, off to the east a little way where the old corral stood, a horse sneezed wearily. Right after, from the shadowed gloom beside a cabin, curt order struck out.

"All right — you can stop right there!"

Cob Jacklyn hauled up, high and wary in his saddle, head swinging, glance probing the dark, trying to exactly locate the speaker. He gambled a question.

"Timberlake?"

"Could be. Name yourself!"

"Cob Jacklyn."

From another angle of darkness came a dry, clipped drawl.

"Over here it's Billings. And wondering why you'd be prowling hereabouts. Why?"

"Looking for Timberlake," Jacklyn replied. "I got a message I promised to deliver to him."

"What kind of a message?" demanded Tap. "And who from?"

"From Lear Morgan."

"Lear Morgan!" There was a short silence. Then Tap exclaimed again, the grind of a quickening anger in his tone. "If you're dragging Lear's name in, just to set up some kind of trick, Jacklyn — !"

"No trick," Jacklyn cut in. "Lear asked me to hunt you up and tell you something. I promised her I would. You want to listen, or don't you?"

"Where'd you get the idea you'd find me here?"

"A lot of people are guessing it so."

There was another pause. Then Tap said:

"All right — I'm listening."

"She said to ask you — if you were tied in with Clay Hanford — to cut loose from him and stay away from him. Understand, she's the one asking this, not me. I told her in my opinion if you were riding with Hanford, you'd stick with him."

"You told her right," Tap said curtly. "What's she trying — something her old man put her up to?"

"Maybe she never said anything of the sort, Tap," put in Frank Billings. "This thing sounds a little bit queer to me. Yeah, a little bit queer. Let's remember who Jacklyn rides for."

"I'm remembering," Tap said grimly.

"Lear's father didn't put her up to anything," said Jacklyn flatly. "If it'll make it any easier for you to understand, I'm not with Crown any more."

"Not with Crown? Why, far back as I can remember, you've been with Crown. Just what are you trying to put over, Jacklyn?"

"A couple of facts. I tell you again, I'm no longer with Crown. And Lear's concern for you is honest. Take it or leave it!"

Tap's reply came a little low and bewildered.

"I'm trying to get used to it. You mean — Lear's worried about me — about something happening to me?"

"I'd say that's about it," Jacklyn answered. "The way things shape up, there's a mean showdown ahead between Hanford and King Morgan and them who run with Morgan. Whoever rides with Hanford can expect the same treatment Morgan intends to hand out to him. It'll be rough. Lear knows this and is afraid for you. You can believe that, or not. Suit yourself."

Jacklyn started to swing his horse around.

"Just a little minute, friend!" It was Frank

Billings again. "I got a gun on you. Now I still can't quite swallow this about you not being with Crown any more. You've been King Morgan's right hand man for a long time — a damn long time."

"True enough," Jacklyn admitted. "I have been, but no longer."

"Why?" Billings demanded bluntly.

"Could be because King Morgan ain't the same man I used to ride for. And I don't like his friends."

Frank Billings ejaculated softly. "Ha! Now I can understand that. You gag, too, over the way Reed Challis died?"

"That's right."

This time, when Cob Jacklyn swung his horse, no one objected. He disappeared in the night, his horse soft-footing it across the damp meadow sod.

He left behind a considerable period of silence. Presently Tap Timberlake remarked his thoughts.

"Seems kinda hard to believe — after him being Crown for so long. And now, all of a sudden, breaking away. Yeah, hard to believe."

"Until you figure the whys," Frank Billings observed succinctly. "A man can go along with something he ain't too fond of for quite a time, hoping that a change for the better will show. When it doesn't, but instead gets worse, then all of a sudden he's fed up — he just can't take no more. Cob Jacklyn is a tough customer in some ways, but he never was the sort to stand for gulching a man from the dark. The way Frenchy LeBard did for Reed Challis. That was the point where Jacklyn had all he could take."

"He rode for Crown, not LeBard," Tap argued.

"True enough. But you heard what he said about King Morgan not being the same man he used to ride for. Well, that figures Morgan is still playing along with LeBard, and when you trail that fence down to the end post it means Morgan is willing to approve what Frenchy did, just to keep him on his side. And Jacklyn, he just don't want any part of such a setup any more."

"You make it sound reasonable," conceded Tap. "Maybe Lear's had all she can stand, too."

"Smart girl, if so," Billings approved. "I tell you, Tap, any time a man persists in going off too far at a wild tangent, he can all of a sudden find himself standing alone. Which is right where King Morgan could damn easy be, one of these days."

"The boys, Price and Lute, they'd never

break away from him."

"Maybe not, and then again, maybe," said Billings. "I wouldn't bet on it. All their lives the old man has done their thinking for them. And because in the main, things have worked out pretty well for them, the boys have been content to go along. But let something hurt them bad enough to start them thinking for themselves, and most anything can happen."

A couple of miles back along the trail to town, Cob Jacklyn again left the trail for the obscurity of some timber shadows, for along the trail ahead came the rush of approaching riders. They passed in the starlight, a full dozen of them, traveling fast, horses blowing, saddle gear creaking, leaving behind to hang in the still, moist air, the acrid taint of equine sweat and body heat.

There was no doubting who they were and where they were going. One of those passing horses had been a strongly marked, black and white pinto that was Price Morgan's favorite mount.

For a little time Cob Jacklyn stayed where he was, held in brooding, bitter thought. Though not openly admitting it, he had all along been hanging on to the hope that perhaps the jolt of his quitting Crown might have brought King Morgan back to earth, to common sense. Vain hope, indeed! The retrogression shaping up in the domineering cattleman was plainly beyond all halting. With King Morgan there was now but one issue. Rule or ruin.

What might have been — what could have been between himself and Crown, Cob Jacklyn now knew would never be. A big chunk of his life — the best chunk — was a thing wasted, thrown away in the interests of one not worthy. A moment of vast and desolate regret — almost a grief — possessed him. Then the man's tough, basic fibre asserted itself, and a cold, fixed anger took over.

He reined to a nearby ridge, set his horse climbing to the crest of it, up where the timber thinned and gave way to starlit open. From such a spot sound would carry far. Mentally measuring time and distance and the speed of riders moving to raid, Jacklyn presently hauled his rifle from its saddle boot, pointed the muzzle to the sky and levered out three spaced shots.

The reports broke the night's stillness wide open, rocketing and reverberating away and away to be lost finally in far, rolling echoes. The shots would, Jacklyn knew, reach many ears, would set some men wondering and trying to translate meaning, while others, like Tap Timberlake and Frank Billings, would be alerted. Which was the thing Jacklyn intended and hoped for — that these two men would not be trapped and caught unawares.

He slid the rifle back into its boot, stepped down, took a coat from behind his saddle cantle, donned it, then squatted on his heels, spinning up a smoke. He had the whole full night to listen through, and the sounds that would come from it would give him the story of its happenings.

Frank Billings's horse, which Clay Hanford had ridden to town, was nothing to look at, but, Hanford decided, on his way back to headquarters, he'd never forked a better trail horse. It was sure-footed and trail wise, with an easy, reaching gait just short of a run, and which covered distance in a surprising fashion. Also, so easily and smoothly did the animal travel, Hanford found himself nodding in the saddle, and he had to shake himself and stretch and stare at the stars to ward off the drowsiness threatening to drug him.

It had been a long and active day. Musing over the events of it, he knew that certain issues had been set in motion which must now work their way to some inexorable con-

clusion which as yet no man could fully pre-
dict.

Drowsiness, persistent and stealthy,
reached for him again, but now was fully
routed when abruptly, out in the night
ahead, a rifle spread three long-running
echoes.

Hanford hauled up short, every startled
sense alert and searching. For some little
time he held right where he was, after which
he swung away from the trail and paralleled
it as he pushed cautiously on.

Five minutes, ten — twenty. With another full mile put behind him, night held
silent with no further alarm. He topped the
almost imperceptible height of ground
beyond which ran the long slope down to
the Fandango Creek meadows. Here he
moved into the full open, with the timber
ridges behind him.

Out yonder lay the Reservation range
headquarters, and out there now a single
shot beat a sullen, thumping challenge.
Swiftly on the heels of this one came another, followed by a rattling scatter of them.
And thin almost to nothingness, lifted a
man's wild, mocking battle howl.

Clay Hanford needed no further evidence
of what was afoot. This was night raid, the
thing he had feared when he advised Tap

Timberlake and Frank Billings to sleep away from the cabin for a time. Now they were out there, valiantly holding the fort, and against long odds by the tempo of the shooting. Hanford slid his newly purchased rifle from under his leg, levered in a cartridge and lifted his horse to a run, driving straight on.

Ahead, gunfire ran a hard, pounding, unbroken racket. Once more came that thin, challenging battle cry, and right after, closer at hand, another voice rolled across the night, shouting a heavy order. King Morgan's voice!

Hanford pulled up and threw two shots that way, knowing it would be blind luck if he hit anything, for he was shooting at a sound, from atop a horse that was whirling and sidling, uneasy from excitement.

Close at hand another voice let out a startled curse, and followed it with a warning yell.

"Behind us! Look out — somebody behind us!"

Hanford drove on, and like a ghostly shadow, a mounted figure went spinning past him. A gun flamed, almost in his face, and he marveled that he was unhit. He hauled hard around, glimpsed the rider in the star glow and snapped a shot. The rider sank from sight, and a horse went racing away under an empty saddle.

Further over another shout lifted. "Adan — Harry Adan — !"

There was no answer and the shout went on, angrily.

"I tell you we rode into something. Those first three shots were a warning. And now they got us between them. Harry Adan — where the hell are you?"

Again Clay Hanford shot at the sound of a voice, shot until his rifle snapped empty, and he had to pause to jam more cartridges through the loading gate.

A few shots came back at him, but now there was uncertainty out there in the hostile dark, and the shooting ran raggedly and began to fritter out. Hoofs pounded, and were suddenly a concerted rush of movement racing away into the night. A single gun remained to blast a final spiteful shot, but when Hanford returned the fire, shooting at the gun flash, it too went silent, and a last tattoo of speeding hoofs faded after the others.

Of a sudden the night was breathless and still.

Hanford spurred on toward headquarters, sending his call forward.

"Tap — Frank!"

It was Frank Billings who answered, a little tiredly.

"Clay! Am I glad you showed up. Come on in."

That tired note sent a swift drift of uneasiness through Hanford. "You hit, Frank?"

"No. But Tap is."

Hanford found Frank Billings on his knees beside a still figure at a corner of the corral. He was swiftly down.

"Not dead?"

"No. But hit pretty bad, I'm afraid. Can't tell for sure until we get him inside with some light. That crowd be back, you think?"

"Not tonight. Give me a hand!"

Hanford eased Tap's limp form into his arms, and with Frank Billings hurrying ahead to get a light going, carried him into the cabin. He eased Tap down on a bunk, and while Billings held the light, made swift examination. Tap had been shot through the body on the right side. He had lost a lot of blood and there was no doubting the seriousness of the wound.

"We'll do what we can," Hanford said. "Past that he's got to have a doctor. Where's the closest one?"

"Hendersonville," Billings said. "A damn long way."

"Long way or short, he must have that

186

doctor. In the mean time, is there anybody else — ?"

"They say Hannah Scorry, Mike Scorry's missis, is a good hand at anything like this."

"That will be it, then," Hanford declared. "We'll do what we can, then move him to town to the Ute House."

"A tricky chore, moving him," Billings said. "Should have a wagon, and we ain't got any. Maybe we should keep him quiet right here."

Hanford shook his head. "Won't do, Frank. Like I said, that crowd won't be back tonight. But, King Morgan, being the sort he is, they'll be back again before too long. And when they do, this will be no place for a sick, wounded man. I'll get a wagon. I'll borrow one from Hack Williamson. There's a clean shirt in my saddlebags. Dig it out and tear it up for bandages. And we'll need some hot water —"

Half an hour later, Hanford straightened up and pulled a blanket over Tap Timberlake. He had done the best he knew how. He had washed the wound, front and back, and bound compresses in place. Now it was up to the luck of the future and the reservoir of strength in Tap's lean young carcass. Looking down at Tap's still, drained face, Hanford knew a gust of affection for this cheerful, happy-go-lucky rider.

In building up the fire to heat water, Frank Billings also brewed a pot of coffee, and now he silently handed Hanford a steaming cup. Hanford put away half of it, then spoke thoughtfully.

"First hint I had of anything breaking was back along the trail when somebody turned loose three shots. What at, I don't know — but not at me. But there wasn't any more shooting until I came out into the creek meadows. I still can't figure the three shots — why they were and where they were."

"Those three shots put Tap and me on our toes," Frank Billings said. "We were set and waiting when the raiders hit. Surprised 'em some, I think, to find us waiting for them. Then, when you hit 'em from behind, they had a bellyful — quick!"

Hanford downed the rest of his coffee.

"We won't be that lucky again. And I'm no way happy over pulling you and Tap into trouble like this."

Billings shrugged. "You didn't pull us into anything. We moved in of our own accord. It was all or nothin' for both of us, which we knew full well. And what do you think of this? A while after you left for town, Cob Jacklyn rode in."

"Cob Jacklyn! Peaceful?"

"Peaceful. Brought a message for Tap — from Lear Morgan."

"What kind of message?"

"Wanting Tap to cut loose from you."

"Another King Morgan try to weaken me down, eh?" Hanford's tone ran harsh. "Jacklyn had a hell of a nerve, coming in here with that kind of talk. Wish I'd been here."

"Wasn't all he had to say," went on Billings. "Said he told Lear Tap wasn't the quittin' sort, that now he was with you, he'd stick, no matter what. And damned if Jacklyn didn't sound like he found satisfaction in that fact. Then, to wind it up, he said he'd quit Crown."

"Quit Crown! You don't mean it."

"That's what he said," Billings averred. "And he said King Morgan was no longer the kind of man he once rode for, and that he couldn't stomach Morgan's friends. Meaning in particular, Frenchy LeBard."

"You think he was telling the truth?" Hanford demanded.

"I do. And I think it was him who let off those three shots as a warning."

Hanford spun a cigarette, staring straight ahead in thought. Presently he nodded, almost imperceptibly.

"You know, Frank — after Reed Challis

189

was slaughtered the way he was, Mike Scorry looked King Morgan in the eye pretty damn stern and defiant. And tonight, when I was buying a rifle from him, Joe Gorman said a couple of things that hinted maybe he was tired of being shoved around by the Morgans, too. Hack Williamson definitely told Morgan off. Now, with Jacklyn quitting Crown, it would seem that a lot of people have had a big plenty of Morgan weight. And losing a man like Jacklyn sure ain't making Crown any stronger."

He went back over to Tap, listened to his breathing, laid a palm on his forehead.

"Fever's beginning to show. We got to have that doctor. What time does the Hendersonville stage pull out of Morgan Junction?"

"Early. Right about the first break of daylight. Has to, to make it there and back before dark."

"I'll see that it brings that doctor," Hanford said.

NINE

Some half mile short of the Reveille Gap road, Price Morgan, who had been slumping lower and lower in his saddle, suddenly gave a moist, gurgling sigh and slid headlong into the black shadows close to the earth. His horse shied away, ramming into another rider who exclaimed sharply.

"Hey! What the hell?"

Right after, he sent a hard call forward.

"Hold up, ahead! We got a man down —"

They had been riding loosely bunched, these men who had ridden on night raid, keeping to no set order save that King Morgan was in the lead. The rest had been shifting back and forth, silent and savage with the frustration of defeat. So now, halted by this call of alarm, none were certain just who the down man was.

King Morgan's reply came back sharply.

"Who is it? What's the matter with him? Mastick, have a look!"

Speck Mastick, new foreman of Crown since Cob Jacklyn quit, left his saddle, softly swearing. He dropped on one knee and snapped a match. The light of it flickered a brief moment and went out. Mastick's mumbled cursing quieted and his tone was subdued as he called.

"It's Price!"

"Price!"

The word was almost an eruptive cry as King Morgan came wheeling back. He swung heavily down and crouched beside Speck Mastick. His hands sought the prone figure, pulling, turning that figure over.

"Price! Talk to me! Price — what's wrong? What — ?"

These first anxious words ran out, replaced by others that were hoarse and strained.

"Let's have another match, Speck?"

Now Lute Morgan was down beside them, as was Frenchy LeBard. This time Mastick had better luck with his match. It flared boldly for a little time — time enough to plainly mark the slackness of Price's face and the soggy, drenched stickiness all across the front of his shirt.

Frenchy LeBard, incapable of true sentiment of any sort, made blurted statement, blunt but factual.

"Hell! There's a dead man!"

It was so.

King Morgan had known it the moment

he laid a hand on Price. Held up by some blind desperation, or unguessed strain of stoicism, Price, with a bullet through his chest, had ridden this far from the scene of attempted raid, dying in his saddle.

Slowly King Morgan got back to his feet, taking an uneven step or two to one side, there to stand rigid, staring blindly into the night, stunned by an emotion he'd about forgotten existed. Grief! A gray, gray blanket of it, shrouding down over him.

Price, his eldest — gone — !

They waited for him, the rest did, mainly in silence, though a few muttered words were traded back and forth. Somebody made one clear statement.

"Harry Adan must have got it, too. He ain't showed."

Lute Morgan, starting to move out beside his father, stopped a couple of strides short, facing the night with his own problem of stunned realization, trying to adjust his thoughts to the bleak, unalterable fact.

Abruptly King Morgan flung a taut arm at the sky, fist clenched, a man making some silent vow for the future. He stood so for a breath or two, then dropped his arm, turned and spoke in a deadened tone.

"Put him on his horse."

Speck Mastick, with Frenchy LeBard and

Buck Siebold helping, did this. They laid Price face down across his saddle and tied him there. They rode on, to strike the Reveille Gap road, then along this to the turnoff leading to Crown headquarters.

They came in across the compound under a sky in which the stars had receded, thus deepening the darkness. These were the black, cold, early morning hours, when the vitality and spirit of men were at their lowest ebb. They lifted Price from his saddle, carried him into the bunkhouse and covered him with a blanket.

"Lute," ordered King Morgan, "stir up the cook. And there's a couple of bottles in the office. Fetch them."

By the time they had unsaddled, lights were burning in the cookshack, and woodsmoke, invisible in the dark, seeped from the cookshack chimney and drifted its acrid scent across the compound. They trooped into the cookshack, gathered about the long, oil-cloth covered table and waited for the coffee to brew up. Lute Morgan brought the whiskey from the office, but did not stay to drink any. Instead, he returned to the ranchhouse, where now a light also burned.

He went through the kitchen into the living room and there faced his sister. Lear was wrapped in a night robe, her feet in house slippers of quilted buckskin. Her hair was in the usual heavy braid between her shoulders, and her eyes, though heavy with sleep, were quickening with perception as she studied his face.

"I heard the horses coming in," she said. "They woke me. Lute, there was a — a raid?"

He nodded, held silent by the enormity of the news he must presently give her; an enormity steadily growing in his own consciousness. It was like a wound, numbed for a time by initial shock, then with the pain biting ever deeper and deeper as shock gave way to increasing realization of bitter reality.

Now she saw the shadow of this thing in his eyes, in the drawn tension of his lips. She came closer to him.

"Lute, you — you're not hurt?"

He shook his head.

"Father?"

"No, Price." He finally found the words.

He saw the fear leap into her eyes. She twisted her hands, and her lips began to tremble.

"B— bad?"

He could only nod, but in that nod she read it all.

"Oh — Lute —!" It was a thin wail, and

195

then her face was in her hands, her shoulders shaking. "I knew it would come to this. I — I knew it — !"

Awkwardly, because it had been long since he had shown her any real gentleness, Lute Morgan dropped a comforting hand on his sister's shoulder.

In the first gray, hesitant light of early dawn, Clay Hanford was in Morgan Junction, watching the Hendersonville stage make up, and giving the driver explicit directions concerning a doctor. Mike Scorry came out of the Ute House with the mail sack, and when the stage left, rocking and creaking on its leather thoroughbraces, Hanford faced the hotel keeper with blunt request.

"To be sure you'll bring him here," Mike Scorry agreed stoutly. "And my wife will do her blessed best by him. For he is a good lad, is Tap Timberlake. A mite harum-scarum, but never mean about it. And just reckless enough to give the devil the back of his hand, any old time. Ay, bring him here. There'll be a room ready and waitin'. Would it be any business of mine how he got shot?"

Hanford sketched the raid briefly. Mike Scorry shook a slow and regretful head.

"They have had their own way overlong,

the Morgans. Now there is no charity or wisdom left in them. Before they are done, they will destroy themselves."

From town, keeping in mind directions given him by Frank Billings, Hanford headed straight for Running W, riding in there under the first flare of sunrise.

The headquarters stood on a little benchland above a bend of Piute Creek. It was an orderly layout, well kept and pleasant to the eye. About the house with its neatness and the touch of color at the windows and the scatter of flowers out front, was the reflection of a feminine touch.

At the corrals, Hack Williamson and three riders were catching and saddling. Williamson came out a little way, showing a quiet friendliness.

"We were about to head for your range. I want to clear it of any strays of mine."

"No hurry about that," Hanford said. "Though you can do me a favor."

"How's that?"

"Loan me a spring wagon and team for a few hours."

"Of course," Williamson said quickly. "Or the buckboard, if it'll be handier."

Hanford shook his head. "The wagon will be best. More room. I got a wounded man to move to town."

"Wounded man?" Williamson's glance sharpened.

"Tap Timberlake. Happened last night, late. A raid was thrown at us."

"King Morgan?"

Hanford nodded. "Among others."

Hack Williamson's jaw line turned solid as he wheeled and called an order.

"Barney, hook a team to the spring wagon." He faced Hanford again, tone running harsh. "Morgan's insane. He must be, to go on like this, trying to deny undeniable fact. The man's feudal, living in another age. You look kind of beat. No sleep last night?"

"None. But that part's all right."

"Hell it is! An honest man is entitled to an honest night's sleep. Come on into the house and have some coffee while Barney gets the wagon ready."

Hanford hesitated, looking over at the corrals. Williamson took him by the arm.

"Come along. At this stage of the game another minute or two one way or the other isn't going to make any difference."

They went into the kitchen where a wave of savory warmth met them. Mrs. Williamson was there. And Moira. Moira in crisp gingham. Moira with the shining ebony head and the lovely violet eyes. With the soft generous mouth, now quick smiling and exclaiming at sight of him.

"Clay! It's good to see you."

"The man's had a rough night," announced Williamson. "He could use some coffee and a quick bite of something."

Molly Williamson reached for the coffee pot, and Moira, almost before her uncle finished speaking, had the frying pan on and bacon sizzling. Also, neither of the women had missed the full import of Williamson's tone and words, and now they looked at him questioningly.

"Morgan, LeBard — that gang," the ranch owner explained. "They threw a raid at Hanford last night. Tap Timberlake got hit. Hanford's taking him to town in our spring wagon."

Molly Williamson exclaimed her concern.

"You could bring him here, Mr. Hanford. I'm fond of Tap. He always seems such a boy."

"So he does, Ma'am," Hanford said. "But in a fight he's plenty man. Obliged for your offer, but I'm figuring on putting him in the hotel in town, where Mrs. Scorry will look after him until the doctor gets here from Hendersonville."

"He'll be in good hands with Hannah Scorry," Molly Williamson admitted.

Moving quietly, Moira had set a place at the kitchen table. Now she broke two eggs into the frying pan and with a spoon began dipping hot bacon grease over them, while soberness replaced the smile on her lips. Soon she deftly slid the contents of the pan on a plate and put this in front of him.

As she did this her shoulder touched his and her dark head was bent beside him, and there was a freshness and a fragrance about her that sent a sharp gust of revitalized feeling through him. Much of the night's weariness seemed to suddenly lift. Glimpsing her hands he made a discovery. On neither of them was a ring.

He pondered this while he ate. Finished, he reached for his smoking and got to his feet. To Molly Williamson he said:

"Ma'am, I'm obliged. You're mighty kind."

Hack Williamson went out ahead of him. Moira walked to the door with him, dropped a hand on his arm, looking up at him very gravely. Her eyes were so clear it seemed he could almost see himself in them.

"These are bad days, Clay," she said with simple concern. "You must be very careful."

He dropped a hand over the one on his

arm. "I notice something missing."

She colored, but her glance held steady. "Some day I may explain all that to you."

He went on to where the spring wagon and team now waited. To Hack Williamson he said, "I'll leave the roan here until I bring the wagon back."

From the open door, Moira watched the wagon and driver drop down the low slope of the benchland and funnel out across the quarter mile of open into the timber beyond. When she turned away she found her aunt regarding her with a gently admonishing eye.

"However much you feel in his debt, my dear, I'd remember that he is still a virtual stranger. Until I knew him much better, I would not let my interest grow too great."

Moira flushed again, but her quiet answer was firm.

"I feel I've known him a very long time, Aunt Molly. It is like Clay himself said. No two people can go through the kind of experience we did together, and ever feel like strangers again. Somehow a lot of time, a lot of years were bridged when Clay Hanford pulled me out of Piute Creek and carried me to safety."

"Yet," pointed out Aunt Molly, with fine feminine intuition and perspicuity, "that man stands behind a high barrier of reserve. Perhaps not consciously, but definitely. I sensed it in Gorman's store, night before last. I sensed it in this very room. Our sex is being held in constant judgment by Clay Hanford. He might be kind, he might be gentle, and is probably both. Yet he stands remote. Sometime, somewhere, another woman has hurt him, hurt him wickedly."

Moira's dark head nodded slow agreement. "I have felt that, Aunt Molly."

"Also," went on Molly Williamson, "I too, notice something missing. Where is Lute Morgan's ring?"

"In my room," Moira said steadily. "I am returning it the next time I see him."

"Because of Clay Hanford?"

Moira considered a sober moment.

"Partly. Partly because of Lute himself."

Molly Williamson waited for further explanation, which presently came.

"Not because of Clay as an individual, or the manner in which we met. But because of what he represents. And that is an issue that seems to have brought matters to a head, here in Fandango Basin — an issue that is forcing the Morgans to show their true colors.

"I've always intended to return Lute's ring, Aunt Molly. Because it has never really counted in the way such a ring should. Yes, I'd have given it back long ago, except that I did not want to stir up a quarrel. I knew Uncle Hack was trying his best to get along with King Morgan, and I did not want to do anything which might start trouble. But now that Uncle Hack has taken his stand, I'm going to take mine."

"It will still be an unpleasant moment, I'm afraid," Aunt Molly said.

"Yes, it will be," Moira agreed. "But no matter."

At Reservation headquarters, Frank Billings heard the wagon coming in across the creek meadow and stepped to the door as Hanford braked to a stop. Hanford's first words were of concern.

"How is he?"

"About the same. Mike Scorry had no objections?"

"None. There'll be a room ready and waiting. Everybody, it seems, likes Tap. Mrs. Williamson wanted me to bring him to Running W."

Billings nodded musingly. "Being the grand kind she is, she would."

They padded the bed of the spring wagon with blankets, then carefully carried Tap Timberlake out and placed him on them. Tap was still unconscious, and his thin, boyish features burned with fever. They covered him with blankets and propped the rolled up bulk of still more about him so that he would ride steady and in as much protected comfort as possible. Ready to leave, Hanford turned to Billings.

"Some facts we might as well face, Frank. Morgan will be back. Maybe not tonight, or tomorrow night or a week from now. But one night he will. And we can't hope to hold this headquarters every time against the odds the way they are now. Our only chance is to siwash it, to keep them guessing where we are, and to hit them in our own way and in our own good time.

"So, load up that pack horse of yours. Put Tap's saddle on his bronc and use it to carry stuff, too. You know this country. Throw down a camp somewhere that's reasonably hidden, and then, toward evening, drift into town. I'll be there, waiting for the doctor's report on Tap. All right with you?"

Frank Billings nodded quickly. "I was ready to suggest something of the sort, myself. We got to work the odds down some way before we try a full out stand, now that we know for sure how rough Morgan and his crowd intend to play. See you in town."

It was noon before Hanford brought the wagon in at the Ute House. For he had traveled slowly and with great care, coming in from headquarters, and miles so traveled had eaten up time. Mike Scorry was there to help carry Tap in to a room, and Hannah Scorry took over immediately, exclaiming her concern. She was a gaunt, big-boned, red-headed woman, a trifle on the blowsy side, but deft and gentle and enormously capable on such an occasion. She ordered Hanford and her husband out of the room and called in a half-breed maid of all work to help her.

Mike Scorry led the way into the barroom and set out bottle and glasses. Hanford downed a solid jolt of whiskey, for of a sudden, he was deeply weary. And it was good to lean against the bar on propped elbows and feel the warmth of the whiskey steal all through him, relaxing and taking away some of the strain of fatigue. Mike Scorry eyed him gravely.

"In young Tap yonder you know the damage that came to you, last night. But have you any idea of what you gave in return?"

Hanford shook his head. "Not for sure. I thought I might have put one of them out of the saddle, but I wouldn't want to bet on it. Things were happening fast and the starlight was tricky."

"King Morgan," said Mike Scorry, with slow deliberation, "has reason to mourn greatly. His eldest was killed."

Hanford's head jerked up. "His eldest? Price! You mean, Price took a bullet?"

"Ay. And Harry Adan, one of Frenchy LeBard's riders — he's missing, too."

"How did you hear?"

"From Speck Mastick. I was at Joe Gorman's getting some groceries for my kitchen. Mastick drove up in the Crown buckboard, after a big list of supplies. Seems he's foreman out there now, what with Cob Jacklyn gone. Always a mouthy sort, now that he's foreman, Mastick acts like he's nine feet high. He had plenty of threat talk over what's to happen to you, and along with that, Joe and me got Crown's side of last night's ruckus."

Clay Hanford shook his head in a slow and somber regret.

"I'm sorry," he said simply. "Sorry as hell. King Morgan had a family. A girl, two boys. Could have been a fine, tight circle. Something to be cherished and protected carefully at all costs. Now the circle is broken. And no matter what happens from here on in, even if he puts me six feet under and ends up owning all of Fandango Basin from the Smokies to the Greystone Hills,

Morgan still loses. Things will never be the same for him. He'll never get out from under the weight of what it has cost him. Why can't a man be satisfied with enough? Why must he always want more?" Hanford shook his head again.

"It is to be regretted," Mike Scorry agreed. "Yet it is not King Morgan for whom I am sorry. Not even for Price, who was his father all over again. There was no sorrow in either of them for Reed Challis, a good man that I and Joe Gorman and Pete Garth and a few other town folk laid away yesterday. Nor would they know any sympathy for Tap Timberlake. It is for Lear I know my regret, and perhaps a bit for Lute. As my Hannah has said more than once, it is God's own wonder Lear has turned out as well as she has, all things considered. For she's little more than a youngster."

The hotel owner paused to pour a second drink, then went on.

"Ay, you are sorry, and I believe it. But this is not your fault. You have every right to fight for what is lawfully yours. You'd be a fool to let regret weaken your purpose."

"I don't intend to let it," Hanford said quietly. "But I still wish it might be otherwise." He put away the second drink, then spun up a smoke. "I'll be around again this

207

evening. I want to get the doctor's report on Tap. Obliged for everything."

Mike Scorry shrugged.

"You owe me nothing, yet. It could be you never will. For that I will wait and see."

Out front, Clay Hanford untied the team and climbed into the spring wagon. As he did so a rider swung into the street and came jogging. It was Cob Jacklyn, and he pulled in at the Ute House rail beside the wagon.

Hanford studied the former Crown rider guardedly. Always a neat man, Cob Jacklyn now had a slightly seedy look to him. His leathery cheeks stood in need of a razor and he had the all-over look of having slept the night in the brush. He showed neither interest in Hanford, or animosity toward him. On pure impulse, Hanford spoke.

"By any chance, Jacklyn, could you have fired three shots last night, out toward Reservation range?"

Jacklyn had stepped from his saddle and was loosening the latigo a trifle. He looked across his saddle at Hanford, without showing the slightest break of expression. He was silent so long, Hanford figured he'd get no answer and he gathered up the reins and was about to kick off the brake when Jacklyn responded curtly.

"I might have. Why?"

"Wondering," said Hanford. "Wondering just where you stand?"

"By myself." With this, Jacklyn wheeled and went into the hotel.

Leaving town, Hanford let the team make their own pace. He thought of what Mike Scorry had told him and turned the implications of it over in his mind. Price Morgan — dead! A Sixty-six rider by the name of Adan, missing. Dead men, wounded men. With the issue just begun.

He considered the enigmatic words of Cob Jacklyn and out of all of it arrived at no definite certainty beyond the one that his arrival in Fandango Basin had triggered an eruption of events that were growing increasingly grim and far-reaching, in a world gone savage.

It did not look like that kind of a world. All around was freshness and vigor, every slope, every meadow. Under a faultless sky, timber glinted in the sunlight, and out of its warmed tops the spicy fragrance of resin drifted down. A still world, and seemingly a peaceful one. But this face of it was false.

The team jogging in front of Hanford had traveled this road between Running W and town many times, and knew every inch of it. They did not need to be driven, just allowed their heads. Once they slowed to a near stop, to let a file of cattle cross the road, all Running W stuff, for this was the heart of Hack Williamson's range. Further along the road dipped to cross the gravel of a little wash, and here was water and the team stopped, heads tossing. Hanford rode the brake to keep the wagon from running up on the horses, slacked off the reins and let them drink.

They did so, leisurely, pausing a time or two to look around while they rolled their bits and let water dribble from their lips. Presently, of their own accord, they tightened the traces and went on, leaning into the short upward pull of the wash. Immediately beyond the rim of this, Hanford again set the brake and hauled up on the reins. Facing him from the saddle, not twenty yards distant, was Lute Morgan.

Alertness surged through Hanford, bringing him high and erect on the wagon seat, right hand swinging free past the gun at his hip.

"No!" cried Lute. "Nothing like that! No need of it."

His words were taut, strained, but in no way challenging.

He came ahead, even with the wagon, and leaned forward in his saddle. And now his words were another thin cry.

"Why in hell did you have to come to Fandango Basin?"

Hanford watched him guardedly and with growing wonder. Lute's face was twisted, but with other emotions than anger. Stripped of all semblance of his former swagger and arrogance, he seemed startlingly young and bewildered. Like one now faced with brutal facts he'd never conceived would come his way, who had taken his first real whipping from the inexorable realities of life, and was left lost and uncertain and stung with grief.

Hanford spoke quietly. "I'm sorry about Price. I never wanted anything like that to happen. I asked only to be left alone."

Lute sagged back in his saddle and now his words turned dull.

"Price is only part of it — just part of it."

Hanford nodded. "Only part of it. For right now Tap Timberlake lies in the Ute House, a bullet through him, waiting for a doctor from Hendersonville. Did Tap ever do you or any other Morgan a harm, Lute? No, he never did. Now here's something you should take home with you, something for you to make your father understand. No man ever yet set himself up as God — and made it stick! It's up to you to make him realize that, before what's already bad, can get a hell of a lot worse. I say again, I'm sorry about Price. I'm sorrier about Tap. And it was all so damned unnecessary!"

Lute stared somberly at Hanford, then past him.

"Yeah," he mumbled, in that same dull, numbed way, "yeah, that's it. Unnecessary — so damned unnecessary. All of it."

With the words he dug in the spurs and lifted his horse to a lunging run, clattering down into the wash and across it and away along the road beyond.

Hanford drove on, pondering the strangeness of Lute Morgan's words and actions. It was fairly obvious that Lute had been to Running W.

Breaking into the long clearing of the Piute Creek meadow, the team picked up their pace, near home and rest now, and anxious for it. An old rider with a crooked leg limped into view and waited for Hanford to pull up at the corrals. He took over the reins and began unhitching the team without comment. Hanford looked around.

"I'd like to thank Hack Williamson for the loan of the rig and team."

"Boss ain't here just now," the old rider said. "I'll tell him."

Hanford's roan was tied to the corral

fence. He went over, tested the cinch, set up on it a trifle, freed the reins and stepped into the saddle. For a moment he sat, looking across the interval to the ranchhouse. It was quiet and still, no one in sight. Knowing a faint touch of disappointment he swung the roan and rode off.

Half angrily he tried to close his mind against the cause of this disappointment, then shrugged and silently admitted it. He had hoped for another glimpse of Moira Williamson.

Back a full mile toward town, he left the road and cut away to the slow lift of a timber ridge, climbed this until he found a quiet clearing where the sun struck warmly through. Here he off-saddled, spread his saddle blanket, lay back on it, tipped his hat over his eyes and went to sleep.

TEN

He awoke to the consciousness that he was not alone.

The sun beat warmly upon him and a lazy stir of wind, playing in the timber tops, sent down a faint sighing. In the distance a Stellar jay lifted its slightly raucous, though not unmusical call. Closer at hand a pine squirrel scolded. These were the normal sounds of a land's peace and solitude. Yet every instinct told him someone was near.

He cracked an eye. There, seated a few feet away, was Moira Williamson. Her head was bare and she was in tan riding clothes, and in the burnished sunlight it seemed to Hanford with his first waking glance that she was all black and gold. Her arms hugged her knees and her head was tipped back, her lips slightly parted as she watched the pine squirrel in its scolding from the safety of a lofty limb. She was thoroughly in tune with her surroundings, a girl without pretense or falsity of any kind, owning only a fine, un-spoiled naturalness to heighten her beauty.

He had these few good moments to watch her. Then the impact of his regard suddenly registered and her head turned and she met his glance. Hanford pushed up on one elbow, drawling.

"I sensed someone around, but when I saw it was you, I could hardly believe my eyes. How did you find me?"

She colored warmly, but her words ran steady.

"Easy enough. Your horse was the last one down the trail. All I had to do was follow the sign. I'm sorry I woke you. But this should serve as a warning that you be more careful. I could have been someone else."

He sat up and reached for his smoking.

"That's right, what with people riding here and there. Like Lute Morgan. On my way back to Running W with the wagon I met up with him."

She nodded, showing no surprise. "I thought you must have, and I worried over what might have come of it. It was one of the reasons I followed you. When you were at the ranch, why didn't you come over to the house to report?"

"Nobody seemed to be stirring. And as far as Lute and I were concerned, there wasn't a thing to worry about. Not a lick of swagger or bully-puss left in that boy. He acted like he'd taken a whipping and couldn't figure quite how it happened." Hanford paused a moment to lick his cigarette into shape. "Yes, he was pretty beat down. I felt halfway sorry for him."

Moira leaned impulsively. "I like you for that, Clay. He seemed so crushed by everything. He said he rode out to our place because he just had to have somebody to talk to. And then, to top it all off, I gave him back his ring. I thought he'd be unpleasant about that. He wasn't. He just seemed a little more crushed. I felt sorry for him, too."

Hanford scrubbed a reflective hand across a whisker-stubbled jaw.

"Lute Morgan has had his first real bite at the tough meat of life, and doesn't know how to chew it. For too long he's been traveling in the protective shade of his father's shadow."

"He told me about Price," Moira said, her tone going sober. "Where will this thing stop, Clay?"

Hanford shrugged. "King Morgan and his crowd got the best answer to that. With me it could have stopped before it began. Now —" He shook his head, hardness ringing in his words. "I'll not be driven out!"

"How about Tap Timberlake?" Moira asked. "You got him to town safely?"

"Yes. But he's full of fever — a mighty sick boy. Mrs. Scorry, she took over right away. She seemed to know what she was doing. But I won't feel satisfied about Tap until I hear what the doctor has to say."

Moira came erect, tucking a stray lock of hair behind her ear.

"Remember," she said, "the morning you and I rode through Pinnacle Pass and you had your first look at Fandango Basin? I told you then how it had already been stained with hate and greed. And that sort of thing still goes on." She added, with a little burst of fierceness, "Should it bring hurt of any kind to Uncle Hack or Aunt Molly, I think I'll end up despising the human race!"

Hanford got to his feet to stand beside her. He shook his head.

"That wouldn't prove anything, either. Not that I can see why harm should come to you or yours from an issue being fought out between two other parties, such as King Morgan and me. But it never does to throw everybody into the same class. I know. I've been through that bit of foolishness. The world always goes on, and somehow you go along with it."

He paused, taking a deep drag at his cigarette, reflective thought narrowing his eyes. She watched him, waiting his further words.

"I don't know why I should say this to you, yet for some reason it seems a good idea. Maybe because it gives answer to a question I've seen in your eyes a time or two. I put a lot of faith in a certain person, once. It turned out to be badly misplaced. I thought I was mortally hurt. I find I wasn't. I was prepared to believe all of her sex were like her. And of course I was wrong there, too."

Moira's horse was ground reined a little to one side and now she moved over to it. She caught up the reins and went smoothly into her saddle. From that vantage point she eyed Hanford inscrutably.

"What happened to change your opinion?"

"Knowing you."

Color flagged her cheeks and she spoke in a slightly breathless way.

"I — I'm happy to restore your faith in my sex, Clay Hanford!"

He stood frowning, as if reaching back to recapture some picture out of the past. He shrugged in failure.

"Now there is a strange thing," he murmured. "Nothing is distinct any more. It is as though it hadn't happened, that no one truly existed. What is a man made of when something once seeming so great, can then become as nothing?"

"Because it wasn't truly great," Moira Williamson said swiftly. "Because it wasn't real."

"That must be it," Hanford acknowledged gravely. "Just not truly real. And you, you say you gave Lute Morgan back his ring. Then with you, maybe, it wasn't real, either?"

She held his glance with her usual candid honesty. "No, Clay — that wasn't real, either."

She lifted her reins, and Hanford spoke his quick protest.

"Not as we're just coming to understand each other!"

She shook her head. "For me it is an understanding that needs thinking on. And the next time you need sleep, cover your trail a little more carefully."

She spun her pony into motion and was soon across the clearing and out of sight in the timber.

Mike Scorry moved quietly about the empty barroom of his hotel, troubled in mind and spirit. In his far off lusty youth he had carried a rifle in the Union ranks under

219

General George Meade, and at Gettysburg had faced and helped break Pickett's gallant, but futile charge. The war over, he came west and swung a spiking sledge along endless miles of rails in the building of the Union Pacific.

Rough years, wild years. Years of disaster and triumph, of death for some and survival for others. And they left Mike Scorry with a yearning for some quiet corner in a big and unspoiled land, where he might find solitude and peace for his remaining years. And when Hannah Burke, a sturdy young waitress in a frontier eating house, consented to share future fortune or misfortune, he set out to find that quiet corner.

He thought he had found it, here in Fandango Basin. Now, it seemed, he was wrong. So long, he mused gloomily, as some men could not resist the insidious poisons of greed and envy and the wish to dominate at any cost, there could be no peace or ease across any land.

Watching the change taking place in King Morgan since he first knew the man, Mike had been fearful of just such a day as was now at hand. From a harshly stern, though reasonably fair man, King Morgan had become one who, ever increasingly laid the weight of a ruthless domination over Fandango Basin.

No longer was there any pretense at fairness. Left now only that rapacious, overbearing ruthlessness. Two nights ago, Marshal Reed Challis had been shot in the back by a man King Morgan called friend, and whom he refused to condemn for the act. Now, one of his own sons lay dead, while along the hall in Room Two, young Tap Timberlake was riding a perilous borderline, consumed with the fires of fever and the agony of a bullet's angry path.

Nagged to moodiness by the somber tenor of his thoughts, Mike gave a final polishing swipe to the bar top, then went out on to the hotel porch. Here Cob Jacklyn sat, low in a chair, hat tipped over his eyes. Mike speculated for a little time on this man, too, but kept his own council and laid his troubled glance along the street.

At the north end of town a rider swung into view and it was Lear Morgan who came rapidly along to rein up at the hotel rail. Cob Jacklyn stirred, straightening in his chair to watch her. She dropped from her saddle, circled the end of the rail and climbed the low steps.

Mike Scorry had known and watched this girl grow up from the time she was a leggy, shy, rather wistful youngster of seven or eight. He had often joined his wife in feeling sorry for her, and agreed fully when Hannah declared in her blunt, yet kindly way — "That girl needs a mother."

Furthermore, Hannah Scorry would long ago have offered the warmth of understanding and the comfort of her big arms to Lear, but for the harsh, unyielding barrier of King Morgan.

Lear's first glance was for Cob Jacklyn, and her words were low and accusing.

"You promised you'd warn Tap!"

Spare and still-faced and remote, Cob Jacklyn got to his feet.

"I did warn him. I told him what you told me to tell him. It was like I said it would be. He wouldn't quit. He stood by his hire."

The girl turned to Mike Scorry. Her eyes were full of the strain of grief and worry, but her face reflected startling strength and resolution.

"Tap?" she exclaimed. "How is he? Lute told me he was here — that he was hurt. I want to see him. I want to nurse him."

Mike spoke gently.

"I'd not mislead you, lass. Tap is a very sick boy. My Hannah is doing all she can for him. There'll be a doctor in on the evening stage. But if you'll feel better —"

"Please, Mr. Scorry!"

Mike led the way to the door of the sick room just as his wife stepped out, a pan of water in her hands.

"Hannah," he said, "the lass would help nurse Tap."

Hannah Scorry gave Lear a long, direct look, then nodded.

"There's nothing more we can do for the boy until the doctor gets here. You may sit with him if you wish." Then, as an added thought, "What will your father say about it?"

"I don't know or care," Lear declared with quick emphasis. "What he says or how he feels will never matter to me again!"

Mike Scorry went back to the porch. Cob Jacklyn was still there and standing. A thin cigarette hung at one corner of his lips and he was staring straight ahead, his face fixed and expressionless. Mike Scorry stopped beside him and spoke, half musing, half angry.

"The man could have been great, what with the force and power of him. But he's become a blind, berserk fool. He lost a son, Price — in a raid of his own choosing. Now, in a different way, he has lost his daughter; Lear wants no more of him. She'll be staying a time with Hannah and me. So her horse will need caring for."

Cob Jacklyn's only answer was a nod, but he left the porch, took the rein of Lear Morgan's pony and led it away toward the stage and livery corral.

Mike Scorry watched him go, then lapsed into a bit of his native brogue as he softly spoke, turning back indoors.

"Scorry, there is something on yon felly's mind. There is that! And it is not a thing in which I see any comfort. Instead I wonder, and grow a bit fearful." He paused and shook his head. "I see no peace in this basin."

The afternoon ran away in somnolent quiet. A capful of fleecy cloud gathered at one of the higher points of the Greystone Hills, hovering there for a time like a fluff of cotton. But presently it broke into fragments and vanished, leaving behind a brief flurry of wind to stir the timber about town, after which all was still again. The sun, dipping westward, threw its lances at an ever increasing slant, and sharp-edged shadows gathered on the eastern side of buildings and pushed steadily outward. A coolness moved in and sharpened.

Mike Scorry was at some minor kitchen chore when Cob Jacklyn showed at the door with meager announcement.

"King Morgan is riding in. A couple with

him. Buck Siebold and Speck Mastick. They stopped at the livery corral."

Mike followed Jacklyn out front and had his look. Morgan and Siebold were still astride, but Mastick's horse was under empty saddle.

"What," wondered Mike, "would they be about?"

Jacklyn shook his head, silent. A moment later they both knew. Speck Mastick came out of the livery corral, leading the pony Lear had ridden to town. It had been re-saddled.

"So that's it," said Mike. "He's come after the lass."

"I knew he would," said Jacklyn.

The not too active later years had made physical change in Mike Scorry, but had in no way dimmed the toughness of spirit that had carried him through a bitter war and then down the march of advance of a wild frontier.

"It will be," he said flatly, "exactly as Lear herself wishes. If she would rather stay with Hannah and me, then she shall stay."

"I admire your sentiment," Cob Jacklyn said drily. "But you better have something to back it up."

"I can manage that, too," Mike said.

He went quickly to the barroom and from

225

a shelf beneath the bar, lifted a sawed-off buckshot gun. This he brought and stacked just inside the front door.

With Speck Mastick leading Lear's pony, the three now rode along the street at a walk, King Morgan in front. He wheeled to a stop at the Ute House rail and fixed his hard stare on Mike and Jacklyn.

Some forty-eight hours or thereabouts ago, Mike Scorry had faced King Morgan. And harsh and savagely domineering as Morgan had been then, he seemed doubly so now. He loomed gaunt and heavy in his saddle. Deep lines bracketed the bitter, down-curving line of his lips, and his bloodshot eyes were those of a man consumed with inner torment. When he spoke it was an eruptive growl.

"My girl in there?"

"Ay," nodded Mike.

"Fetch her out!"

"No," Mike said quietly. "It will be as she herself wishes and no other way."

"Fetch her out, or I'll go in after her!" threatened Morgan.

Mike stood his ground. "And you'll not do that, either."

"You want to go in, King, I'll go with you," Buck Siebold said.

"Now I wouldn't try that, Buck," put in

Cob Jacklyn. "You'd never get there."

Jacklyn stood with shoulders flattened against the front of the Ute House, right knee bent and the sole of his right boot pressed against the wall. His thumbs were hooked in his belt and his glance was cool and steady. Abruptly his easy drawl became bleak, brittle command.

"Mastick — quit jiggling around on that horse! And get both hands up where I can see them!"

Speck Mastick folded his hands on his saddle horn, went quite still. Buck Siebold also stayed put, his face going heavy and sullen.

The glance King Morgan threw at Cob Jacklyn was wicked.

"You damned traitor!" he ground out.

"Someday soon," returned Jacklyn steadily, "maybe I'll explain why."

King Morgan cursed and stepped from his saddle, starting up the hotel steps, his intent plain. Mike Scorry reached inside and brought out the sawed-off buckshot gun. He dropped this across his arm and snicked back both hammers.

"You're being foolish, King!"

Morgan stopped. "You wouldn't dare turn that loose on me!"

"Don't gamble I wouldn't. I may be a fat-bellied hotel keeper now, but in my time I've looked at a considerable number of dead men. Looking at another won't turn me inside out."

"You'd deny me the right to speak to my own daughter?"

"Depends," Mike said, "on what you want to say to her."

King Morgan hesitated, head and shoulders swinging from side to side. He, who had for so long only to command, raged at having to bargain, to give reason for any act of his. But that fat, moon-faced man in the hotel doorway had a benignly implacable look about him.

"All right," Morgan conceded. "I want to tell her that I've come to take her home."

"It is my thought that she will not go with you," Mike Scorry said.

"She will when I tell her to."

Mike considered a moment. "It is her right to speak for herself. You will stay here. I'll fetch the lass."

He went to the door of the sick room. Lear Morgan sat beside the bed. Mike beckoned her and she followed him into the hall.

"It's your father," Mike explained. "He is out front. There is something he wants to say to you. I think you should listen to him, and then speak your exact feeling."

"I know what he wants," Lear said. "He wants me to come home. I won't go. I want to stay here, with Tap."

"Why then," said Mike, "you but tell him so and that is how it will be."

She went with him to the door of the Ute House. King Morgan still held his place on the porch steps.

Lear met her father's blood-shot glance. "Well?"

"I'm taking you home," he said. "Come along!"

Here no suggestion of paternal understanding or kindness. Just an order, blunt, harsh and heavy. Lear flushed under the weight of it.

"No!" she said. "If Mr. Scorry will let me, I'm staying here for the present."

"Both Hannah and I said you might," reminded Mike quietly. "We meant it."

Roiling anger flared in King Morgan.

"Let's have no more of this nonsense. Girl — I'm telling you to come along home!"

Lear flared in return.

"Home?" she cried. "You call it home? Well, I don't! A home should have some warmth in it, some feeling of goodness. How long since there was anything of the sort out there? I can't remember. And how long since a truly decent person visited us?

Why haven't they? I'll tell you why. Because they fear us, and hate us, too — that's why. Maybe you like it that way. Maybe you like to be feared and hated. Maybe it makes you feel great and all-powerful. Well, I don't want to feel great and all-powerful. I don't want to be feared or hated. I just want to care for people — good people, and have them care for me!"

She was choked up as she finished, with a mist of tears in her eyes. Watching closely, Mike Scorry saw that these things, as well as her words, were completely lost on her father, who swung his shoulders, restless with an impatient, deepening anger.

"All right," he blurted sarcastically. "You've had your little visit with these good people, as you call them. Now come on home. I'm not going to tell you again!"

Lear stood still and very straight. Her cheeks turned pale and cold. When she spoke, her words fell just as cold.

"You don't understand, do you? You never would." She shook her head. "No, you never would. Even when you look at the face of Price, lying dead back there at that place you call home, you can't truly understand what killed him. Well, I can. Something deadly and terrible killed him, just as it may kill you — and Lute. That something is your blind lust to dominate and rule. And I never want to be near it again!"

She turned and went back into the hotel, the cast of her head and shoulders as definite in impact as a solidly closed door.

King Morgan stared after her, jarred to a momentary stillness. The congestion behind his eyes deepened. Mike Scorry twitched the muzzle of the buckshot gun ever so slightly.

"I told you how it would have to be, King," he murmured. "As the lass wished it, and no other way. So it will do you no good to stamp and bawl. But you should think on what she had to say. Yes, you should think well on that!"

It seemed for a moment that the cattleman would come right at him, buckshot gun or no buckshot gun. Then Morgan whirled and went back to his horse. In the saddle he put his heavy glare on Mike and Cob Jacklyn.

"Good people!" he said thickly. "Good people — hell! I'll show that little fool who the good people are in this basin!"

He spat into the street and used his spurs so viciously that his horse cringed, squatted slightly, then exploded into a grunting run.

Buck Siebold and Speck Mastick sped after him, Mastick swung half around in his saddle as he hauled Lear's pony along.

Mike Scorry sighed, shook his head and lowered the hammers of the buckshot gun.

"That was a dreary thing to watch and listen to. I can't understand that man. He seems possessed."

Cob Jacklyn flipped the dead butt of his cigarette into the street.

"Lear said it all," he observed thinly. "The lust to dominate. It will destroy him."

There was a note of conviction, of certainty in Cob Jacklyn's words more ominous than casual observation warranted. Mike Scorry, about to turn back into his hotel, paused to lay his puzzled glance on Jacklyn. But Jacklyn had already turned away and was dropping down the steps, to head along the street to The Golden.

ELEVEN

Doctor Herman Klaus was a ruddy, shock-headed, barrel-bodied man who cursed violently, sweat copiously, and was thoroughly competent at his profession. His hands were thick and stubby of finger, yet amazingly gentle and deft with probe or scalpel or suture.

Tap Timberlake, half conscious and hazy with fever and weakness, stiffened and went off into deep darkness at the first touch of the probe, a fact which Doctor Klaus profanely approved of, and then did a thorough job on the wound, cleansing, sterilizing and bandaging. He mumbled and rumbled as he worked, as though carrying on a personal vendetta against the devil and all his works. In between these growling outbursts he found time to compliment Hannah Scorry for her efforts and to pat a white-faced Lear Morgan on the shoulder and smile reassuringly at her out of sea-blue eyes from beneath fiercely bristling brows.

Afterward, while cleansing instruments

and repacking them in his satchel, he gave as his professional opinion the word that all would be well with Tap, providing they checked the fever and warded off possible complications. To which end, he proposed to stay on a few days in Morgan Junction to rest and catch up on his sleep. Also, he would thus gain time to gather nerve for the return trip to Hendersonville with a stage whip who, he vowed, sputtering, drove like a thrice-damned crazy man. Anyone, insisted Doctor Herman Klaus with further profane emphasis, who rode that stage, risked at worst a broken neck, or at best, a ruined nervous system.

After which vehement declaration, Doctor Klaus partook of a generous supper, sought the barroom, set up a game of solitaire at one of the tables, and proceeded to profane the place with the smoke of a black and murderously vile cigar. It was here that Clay Hanford found him and introduced himself.

"I'm Hanford. I sent for you, Doctor. Tap was riding in my interest when he was shot. I'll foot all expenses. How is he doing?"

Doctor Klaus shrugged.

"He was, I understand, close to twenty hours without professional care. I was afraid I would find much infection. I did not. The patient is young, strong and clean blooded. There is considerable fever, but under the circumstances, we must expect that. However, he is being faithfully and capably nursed, and I intend to stay handy for a day or two. All in all, I'd say his chances were excellent."

Doctor Klaus pulled deeply and luxuriously at his cigar and sent another gust of smoke blooming. Clay Hanford gasped, then winnowed his way through it, grinning.

"Good God! Doc, I'd like to buy you a real cigar."

"Buy — hell!" said Mike Scorry from behind the bar. "I'll give him one. I'll give him a dozen. How any man of medicine — !" Mike shook his head, at a loss for words.

Doctor Klaus leaned back, chuckling. He held up his cigar and looked at it lovingly.

"My own brand, made especially to my order. All others I have tried are pale imitations, without flavor, without substance. This — this is the ultimate!"

"It sure as hell is something or other," Hanford declared, backing away.

He went out, surveyed the starlit street, then drifted along it. From a shadow pocket by the Golden, Frank Billings reached him with quiet words.

"Over here, Clay."

Hanford joined him in the close dark.

"Tap?" Billings asked briefly.

Hanford told him what Doc Klaus had said and Billings murmured with obvious relief.

"That's good. That's damned good! I think it calls for a drink."

"Yes," Hanford said, leading the way into the Golden.

Pete Garth, slender, dark, impassive of face, tipped a carefully combed head.

"Gentlemen! Frank, it's been a little time since you were in last."

"A little time," admitted Billings. "Meet Clay Hanford, new owner of the Reservation range."

Pete Garth reached a hand across the bar. "Heard of you, Hanford. Whiskey?"

"And leave the bottle out," said Billings. "I'm going to work over your free lunch, Pete."

Garth shrugged. "What it's there for."

Over a couple of whiskies apiece they ate hungrily, and when they were done, Hanford spun an extra half dollar across the bar against Pete Garth's protest.

"Free lunch is free lunch, but a meal is a meal. And Frank and I just had one."

They spun up smokes and drifted out into the street. "You found a camp,

Frank?" Hanford asked.

"And something else," Billings nodded. "I was gettin' ready to pull out from the cabin when I heard a horse blow and stamp. I took a look and there was one with an empty saddle — a Sixty-six bronc. It made me wonder, of course, so I did a little prowling. Back in the meadow a piece I found where a man had been down, and sign where he'd dragged himself over to the creek west of headquarters. I found Harry Adan lying there in the willows. He must have figgered he'd get to water and lay hid until Morgan came back, or something of the sort. But he was hit harder than he knew." Billings paused, then added, "A mean business when a man has to die in the dark like a wounded animal, even if he did ride for the other side."

"Ask King Morgan how mean," Hanford said grimly. "This Harry Adan wasn't the only one either you or me or Tap happened to hit. They got another dead man out at Crown headquarters. Price Morgan."

"Price Morgan!" Frank Billings exclaimed, then brooded a moment before speaking something not greatly different from what Hanford had said to Mike Scorry.

"No matter how this thing comes out

now, King Morgan has already built a private hell for himself."

"What did you do about Adan?" Hanford asked.

"I unsaddled his horse and piled his gear on a driftwood snag close to the body. Figured we could get word to Morgan or some of that crowd on what to look for and where."

"I wonder," murmured Hanford skeptically, "if any of them would have done as much for us?"

Above town a muted murmur of sound became the cadence of running hoofs. Reaching the head of the street these slowed to a jog and a rider came straight along to the Golden. Clay Hanford and Frank Billings eased into the shadows and watched the rider swing in at the rack, step down and go in, spur chains dragging. For a brief moment as he pushed through the saloon door he was outlined against the inner light. Then the door swung shut and there was only the shadowy bulk of the horse at the rail and the sweat-sour reek of its sweat across the night.

"Know that one, Frank?"

"Dave Rich," Billings answered. "From Crown."

"A tough lad?"

"Wouldn't call him so. Probably sent in to scout things."

"Why then," Hanford drawled, "it wouldn't do to disappoint him. And he's somebody to tell about Adan. Let's have a look at him."

They went back into the Golden just in time to catch a statement by Pete Garth.

"Listen, Rich! Don't ask me questions. I don't hear anything, I don't see anything, I don't know anything. You can tell Morgan that."

If Dave Rich had any reply figured for this, he did not utter it, instead coming around to face Hanford and Billings. He eyed them warily, a run-of-the-mill rider, a little gaunt, a little dirty, a little ragged.

"If it's about us you're wondering, Dave, here we are," Frank Billings said.

Rich had no answer to this, either, just sidling toward the door as Billings went on.

"And if they're wondering out at Crown what's become of Harry Adan, they'll find him over on Fandango Creek, maybe three hundred yards west of the old Reservation buildings. His riding gear is piled on a driftwood snag beside him. His horse may be hanging around, or it may have drifted back to Sixty-six by this time. You'll see they get the word?"

At the door, Rich found his tongue. "I'll tell them," he said thinly. Then he slipped through and was gone.

They listened to hoofs swing away from the rack and move up-street. Pete Garth blew on a glass and polished it carefully before making gruff remark.

"He was asking about you two. I'd keep heads up."

Hanford smiled faintly. "For one who doesn't hear, see, or know anything, you do pretty well, Garth."

The saloon owner shrugged. "Reed Challis used to be in and out of my place regularly. He was my friend. I miss him."

"Quite so," murmured Hanford. "I understand. And — thanks!"

They returned to the street, sought their horses, swung north of town, then edged off the road into the timber a little way and hauled up there. After a little wait they heard the rush of massed hoofs along the Reveille Gap road, going into town.

"Would seem Rich delivered the word, all right," Frank Billings observed drily. "They were waiting for him, not too far up the road."

"Yes," Hanford agreed. "Reservation grass is a secondary thing with Morgan now. What he's out to do is even up for Price.

The others will back him because they can't afford to do otherwise. If he wins, they win. If he loses, they lose. My friend, we are now open game!"

Billings considered before summing up bleakly.

"There's no dirtier stand-off than one of out and out bushwhacking. Ordinarily I'd want no part of such. But it is a knife that can cut both ways, and when the issue becomes one of sheer survival, well — !"

They slanted west along a trace which Billings, holding to it unerringly in the dark, named the Lyle Canyon trail. Once they paused, for again came the distant, drumming echo of running hoofs, cutting up behind them toward Reservation headquarters. Later, off there, a crimson glow began to reflect against the night sky, a glow which grew to a peak, held so for a considerable time, then gradually diminished.

"They've burned us out, Frank," Clay Hanford said, softly bitter. "It wasn't much of a headquarters, but it served. Morgan's not backing away from any of the weapons, is he? Well, that kind of business could be another of those knives with two edges!"

In a spring fed glade in the big timber north of Lyle Canyon, they threw down at the camp to which, earlier in the day, Frank

241

Billings had brought and left his own pack horse and Tap Timberlake's saddle pony with their loads of gear.

"It's a good spot," Billings explained. "Tap and me, we've siwashed it here plenty in the past. It's well off the beaten track and about as far away from Crown range as you can get and still remain in the basin. I figure we can sleep reasonably secure."

He stirred up a small blaze and put coffee on to cook. Waiting for this to turn over they hunkered by the flames, silent and taciturn with their thoughts. Afterward they drank their coffee, had a final smoke, and rolled into the blankets under the coldly watchful eyes of the midnight stars.

Back in Morgan Junction, watching from the shadows by the livery corral, Cob Jacklyn had seen Dave Rich ride into town, stop briefly at the Golden and ride out again. Then it was Clay Hanford and Frank Billings who left town together and, not too long after that, King Morgan led a full dozen others into town, making a quick search of it before spurring out again.

When they left, Jacklyn caught and saddled and followed, and later, from the dark edge of the Fandango Creek meadow, heard Morgan shout harsh orders and saw the first flames creep and grow and tower as men touched off every cabin, every old Reservation ruin. Still later, with the raiders long gone and the fires dwindled to just a few guttering flames and all the creek meadow swimming in a fog of acrid smoke, Jacklyn finally reined away and headed back to town.

It was mid-morning when the Running W buckboard rolled in to Morgan Junction with Moira Williamson driving and her Aunt Molly riding beside her. They left the rig in front of Gorman's store and walked on to the Ute House, Aunt Molly reflecting all the white-haired, gracious, kindly charm of her years, Moira buoyant with youth's lovely vitality.

Cob Jacklyn held down a chair on the hotel porch. He had slept in a back room of the stage station, but was now clean shaven and as neat as possible under such circumstances. As Moira and her aunt climbed the hotel steps, he got to his feet and took off his hat, a quiet, spare, still-faced man with shadowed eyes.

Both Moira and Aunt Molly knew Cob Jacklyn by sight, for he had been long in Fandango Basin. They had also heard how he had left Crown only a day or two before. Their interest in this fact, and his quiet courtesy of the moment, drew their attention, their acknowledging smiles, and Aunt Molly's cheerful:

"Good morning!"

They passed on into the hotel and Jacklyn stood as he was for a little time. Then the locked away impassiveness of his face broke suddenly into a twisted bitterness. He pulled his hat low over his eyes and went down street to Gorman's store, moving with the quick stride of one come to some final definite decision. Shortly he returned, carrying a thin sack of supplies to the stage corral. Fifteen minutes later he rode out of town, heading northwest, the supplies and a roll of blankets behind his saddle.

Entering the Ute House, Moira and Molly Williamson met Mike Scorry, who welcomed them cheerfully.

"Mike," Aunt Molly announced, "I've come to see if I can be of any help to Hannah with Tap Timberlake."

"Sure and that is good of you," Mike declared, wagging his head. "It would seem the lad has a fatal charm for women. Already he's had three of them fussin' over him."

"Three!" echoed Aunt Molly. "Who would they be?"

"Well," said Mike, "there's my Hannah.

244

Then there is Sutie, our half-breed girl who helps about the place. And finally there is Lear Morgan."

"Lear Morgan!" It was Moira's turn to exclaim.

"Ay," nodded Mike. "Lear it is. She's been with us since this time yesterday, sittin' at Tap's bedside, watchin' over him. Hannah had to turn a bit cross with her last night to make her get some sleep. Now the lass is back at her vigil again, guardin' Tap faithful. In a way it is a fine thing, but in another it is sad. For Lear has turned against her father. King Morgan has much cause to mourn, what with Price, his eldest, dead — and now Lear putting her back to him."

"King Morgan," said Aunt Molly firmly, "has brought this on himself. I can know sympathy for Lear, but little for him. When did he ever care how much he hurt others?"

From the hallway sounded rumbling Teutonic accents, and then it was Doctor Klaus and Hannah Scorry who came into the room. Hannah cried her surprised welcome, then introduced Doctor Klaus, who rumbled and beamed his pleasure.

"Doctor," Molly Williamson said, "you must have good news of your patient. Else you wouldn't be so cheerful."

"Madame," declared Doctor Klaus gallantly, "I have full cause to be cheerful. First, because the wound is clean and the fever lessened, the patient sleeps and grows stronger. Second, because it is my good fortune to meet so many kind and lovely ladies."

Hannah Scorry sniffed. "Will you but listen to him," she said scoffingly. "For the first part he speaks the truth, sure enough. I myself can see that Tap is much better. For the rest, this man of medicine is so full of blarney you might well think him straight from the old sod." She looped an arm through that of Molly Williamson and reached for Moira. "Come along to the kitchen. I yearn for coffee and a good long talk."

"I wonder," Moira said, "if I might see Lear, first?"

"Of course, darlin'," Hannah Scorry said. "Go right along in."

Moira went softly along the hall and eased open the door of the sick room. Lear Morgan was in her chair by Tap's bedside, huddled a bit wearily, and, in this relaxed moment, somewhat forlorn and pathetic. But at sight of Moira she straightened and got to her feet, chin up and shoulders squared.

Nearer an age than any two others of their

sex in Fandango Basin, Moira Williamson and Lear Morgan had never been as close as this fact might have suggested. They met, they spoke, but always there seemed to rise some barrier beyond which neither could or would advance.

Often had Moira pondered this, seeking an answer. She sincerely felt it was not the result of her own feelings in the matter, nor could she rightly blame Lear, for she knew some sort of basic uncertainty, or sense of insecurity, together with an almost unnatural homelife, had of later years tended to make the girl solitary and withdrawn.

But here was something different than just another reflection of Lear's usual mood. Here was defiance and challenge, defending something that was hers. A rush of understanding came to Moira, and she smiled mistily.

"Tap — the doctor says he is going to be all right, Lear. I'm so happy for both of you."

Lear stared, as though not quite understanding. When she spoke her words were hesitant.

"Happy — for Tap — and me?"

"Of course," Moira nodded. "For Tap and you. That's the way it is, isn't it? You and Tap? That was the way it used to be, wasn't it?"

Lear's answer was hardly above a choked whisper.

"Yes — yes. Tap — and me. We rode together. He was so good to me — so kind —"

She couldn't go on, for her face was working and abruptly her hands were over her face and she was racked with tearing sobs. Moira went quickly to her and held her in her arms.

There had been a great deal of grief and loneliness, of uncertainty and fear in Lear Morgan. Now it came storming out as Moira held and comforted her.

Gradually Lear quieted and drew back and looked through the dregs of her tears.

"Why are you — so good to me?"

"Good to you! We're friends, aren't we?"

"Friends!" Lear spoke the word softly, some of the tautness leaving her face. "Friends!" she murmured again, as though scarce believing. "A real friend — ?"

"If you'll let me be, Lear." Moira felt she was comforting a lonely, frightened, seeking child.

Lear dropped back into her chair, caught Moira's hand and pressed it against her cheek.

Out at Crown headquarters, King Morgan was putting together the tools for a final drive for revenge and dominance.

There could, he knew, be no halfway measures. So long as one man was able to oppose and defy his authority, then that authority was not complete. And it had to be complete to endure. It was a thing which had to be all or nothing.

Last night he had touched a match to Reservation headquarters, burning it to the ground. And from now on, until cornered and destroyed, Clay Hanford would know neither peace, rest, or security. Which, Morgan vowed implacably, was the way it would be. Afterward, the fools in town would be kicked into line, and such as Hack Williamson, out at Running W, shown who it was that threw the long, wide shadow across Fandango Basin.

This morning, King Morgan had overseen the burial of two men. One was his son, Price. The other, a rider of Frenchy LeBard's, by name Harry Adan. At no time had Morgan shown visible sign of emotion. Stony-faced, stony-eyed, he growled orders other men leaped to obey.

They were all there. Frenchy LeBard, Buck Siebold, Rusty Acuff and their riders. And all of Crown. And of all these, only one person had dared face King Morgan with a differing opinion. It was Lute Morgan who looked his father in the eye and told him he was wrong, that he'd been wrong from the first.

The previous night had been a very long one for Lute Morgan. He had ridden with the rest out to Reservation headquarters and watched the burning of it. But he had struck no match and found no satisfaction in the affair. Back home again, while his father and the others spent the balance of the night in the cookshack, drinking black coffee and waiting for another day to break, Lute found the hours sleepless ones for himself, too.

Alone in the ranchhouse, he prowled it from end to end. The emptiness of it was frightening. Here was nothing except the hollow echo of his own footsteps. He looked at the bunk that had been Price's. He went into Lear's quarters and viewed the various evidences of her past occupancy with a strange sense of humbleness. Feminine oddments, here and there. A touch of color. An eye-pleasing balance in the way the furnishings were placed, and an orderliness found no where else about the place.

Where was Lear now? In town at the Ute House, helping nurse Tap Timberlake. Defying her father, defying his authority. Courageously following her heart and her instinct for what was right and decent.

Lear and Price — both gone. Why? Morgan arrogance, Morgan madness? Rule or ruin. . . .

Lute shook his head wearily, took something from his pocket. A ring, its stone reflecting glints of light. He turned it over and over, staring at it. Once it had graced the finger of Moira Williamson, or was it that her wearing it had graced the ring! In any event, it was no longer there.

What, in the first place, had been his true sentiments concerning the ring? Had he been thoroughly honest, or had he used the ring to assert a possessiveness, as a badge of fancied superiority? More Morgan arrogance, perhaps — ?

Yes, a long, long night. And somewhere along the cold, somber hours of it, Lute Morgan grew up.

So now, here in the taut atmosphere of the morning, he faced his father and gave his opinion. An opinion that this thing should be called off before complete ruin came down on everyone. Also, he declared, for himself he would not ride after Clay Hanford. He would live and let live. And in his words lay an unspoken plea that his father do the same.

But King Morgan merely looked at him as though from a great distance. Speck

Mastick, coming out of the bunkhouse from some final hurried errand, caught the words, stared sneeringly at Lute for a moment, then spat contemptuously at his feet. Which unlocked everything that had piled up in Lute.

He caught Mastick by the arm, spun him around and knocked him flat.

Speck Mastick was as tall as Lute, and heavier. He came back up, raging. And Lute leaped to meet him, toe to toe. It was savage and elemental, no quarter asked, no quarter given. Speck Mastick was driven by blind rage, Lute by the consciousness of a new-found stature and self-respect. And King Morgan watched, stony-eyed, stony-faced, making no attempt to stop it.

Both men went down, both came back up again. But it was Lute who carried the fight, driving in relentlessly, and presently it was Speck Mastick who began giving way. Lute followed his man almost halfway across the compound before nailing him with a rifling fist that put him down again. This time, Speck Mastick stayed down.

Lute turned away, none too steadily. Laboring breath burned raw in his lungs and the muscles of his legs were cased with lead. His face was numb where Mastick's fists had landed. Sweat blurred and scalded his eyes and blood seeped from his lips. But he flung a challenge, harsh and thick, across the compound.

"Anybody else? Any of the rest of you brave bloodhounds want to try your luck? All right then, damn you, don't try sneering at me!"

They didn't answer, none of them, just sat their saddles stolidly, as he marched past them into the ranchhouse kitchen. King Morgan alone swung his head to watch Lute, and for a brief moment something almost like pride gleamed in the cattleman's bitter eyes. Then this gleam flickered out, as if a door had been closed, and a growling order sent a couple of hands to get Speck Mastick back on his feet and help him wobble to his horse and get into his saddle.

After which they rode out, and from a ranchhouse window Lute watched them go. It was on the high, heavy back of his father that Lute's gaze centered and lingered, while a gust of regret held him still and sad.

TWELVE

The headquarters of Frenchy LeBard's
Sixty-six layout consisted of one fair sized
cabin, two smaller ones, a three-sided feed
shed and a single corral. The place was
sprawling and unkempt. The buildings were
raw-boarded, weather bleached and warped,
the fence of the corral patched and propped
in several places where it had begun to sag. In
the corral some half dozen head of saddle
stock dozed and stamped and switched at
flies. All round about the scrambled, broken
country of the Smokies threw a tangle of
slope and gulch and cramped flats, sparsely
grassed over the lower reaches, raggedly timbered along the higher ones.

At the mouth of a gulch the snout of a small
wooden trough dribbled water into a rusty
wash tub, the overflow from this carried by
ditch across a corner of the corral, then left to
lose itself in a soggy flat further along. From
the stove pipe which stuck a rusty length
above the shake roof of the largest cabin, a
thin haze of wood smoke winnowed.

A man stepped into view, carrying a water bucket. He shuffled over to the end of the trough, held the bucket under it, and while the bucket filled, looked listlessly around. He was small and tight faced, in a dirty undershirt and equally dirty, faded jeans that were too large for him and hung precariously at his hips. The limp stub of a Durham cigarette sagged at one corner of his thin, mean mouth. As he started back to the cabin, the weight of the filled and dripping water bucket pulled him over until he seemed to limp as he went along.

From the shelter of a timbered point, Clay Hanford and Frank Billings surveyed the layout below.

"That's Pikey Stent," Billings said. "He does the cooking and general roustabout chores for LeBard. Looks like he's the only one around. What do you think?"

Hanford shrugged. "I'm remembering a few things about Frenchy LeBard. He shot Reed Challis in the back. He's been rustling J P cattle that were mine. Night before last he was certainly with King Morgan in the raid on us, for one of his own men was left behind as evidence. I see no reason to doubt that he was with Morgan again last night when they burned us out. So — !"

"That's it," murmured Frank Billings.

"That's it — exactly! Come on!"

They dropped swiftly down the slope, hauled up before the larger cabin. The thin, tight face of Pikey Stent showed at the door. His somewhat rheumy eyes widened. He made a furtive reaching move, but halted it dead under the harsh impact of Hanford's words.

"Don't try anything! Come out here!"

Pikey shuffled into full view.

"Where's LeBard?" Hanford demanded.

Pikey twitched his thin shoulders.

"Crown, I guess. Least ways, thet's where he went yes'tiday. Ain't been back since."

"Coony Ells?"

"He's with Frenchy."

"Then," put in Frank Billings, "unless LeBard has done some mighty recent hiring, Pikey's all that's here."

"Make sure," Hanford said.

Frank Billings made swift survey of the other two cabins. He pushed past Pikey into the larger one. He came out shaking his head. He was carrying an ancient Henry rifle, with a stock once broken, now wired together. He slammed the Henry against a corner of the cabin and now it was broken again, and useless.

"Nobody else," he said.

Hanford fixed Pikey with a bleak stare.

"You bunk in this cabin?"

Pikey's eyes widened again, with a rising uneasiness.

"Yeah. Sa-ay — what you fellers up to, anyhow?"

Hanford dropped from his saddle. "Going to prove the worth of the old saying about a knife cutting both ways. Or, if that don't fit, we'll make it an eye for an eye!"

Pikey's uneasiness was swiftly greater and he swallowed nervously.

"You must be this feller Hanford?"

"That's right. Hanford it is."

"Well," hurried on Pikey, "I never did nothin' to you. I never saw you before, and I never done nothin' to you. I don't mix in any of Frenchy's quarrels with anybody. I just cook and do chores —"

"Sure, sure," Hanford cut in. "I know how it is. If you got any gear, you better start gathering it."

Now Pikey understood. He wheeled back into the cabin and Hanford followed him.

Here was clutter and unsavoriness. The air was rancid from stale cooking odors, stale human odors. Coming into such out of morning's fine, clean air, Hanford knew a swift distaste. He eyed a stove thick-coated with rust and grease. He jammed a boot heel against the side of it and straightened

257

his bent leg. The stove toppled with a crash, letting down a couple of lengths of stove pipe and a cloud of soot. Live coals, spilling from the open fire box, lay like evil eyes and around them the dry, scuffed floor boards began immediately to darken and send up little filaments of smoke.

The racket made Pikey Stent jump nervously and hurry his efforts at stuffing frugal belongings into a ragged warbag. He jammed a floppy old Stetson on his head, gathered his warbag under one arm and a hodgepodge of gear under the other and headed for the door.

"Hell of a note!" he complained shrilly, "This is Injun stuff, burnin' a man out."

"That's what I thought last night when I saw my place going up," Hanford retorted bleakly. "But I didn't write the rules of this fight."

The smoke about the spilled coals thickened, and then there were little fingers of pale flame flickering and growing quickly larger. A minute pitch pocket in one of the floor boards snapped with a faint spitefulness. It wouldn't, Hanford knew, take long.

Outside, Pikey Stent stood as though unsure just what to do.

"You got a saddle," Hanford asked.

Pikey nodded. He had a saddle.

"Then go cinch it on one of those broncs in the corral. Because we're turning the rest loose."

Frank Billings had been busy in the other two cabins. Smoke was seeping from their open doors. Pikey Stent headed for the corral at a shuffling run. Over and over he kept shrilling: "Hell of a note — hell of a note!"

They watched him catch and saddle and tie on his gear. They turned the rest of the saddle stock into the open. Then Frank Billings dropped a blazing sulphur match into one of the feed shed mangers half full of remnants of wild hay. Almost instantly flames began to climb. They got into their saddles and rode back up the slope, leaving Pikey Stent to his own devices.

Uncertainty still gripped Pikey. Up to a very few minutes ago his world had been fairly stable. To be sure, it was a slovenly, uninspiring, meagrely frugal one. Yet it was a world which Pikey thoroughly understood and was satisfied with. Now it had come apart right before his eyes. Pikey hadn't been half a mile from this spot in the past six months. He was like a bird finding the door of its cage suddenly opened, and was fearful over leaving. But leave he did, finally, as flame broke through the roof of the feed shed and began to tower. There was a trail leading east and south. Pikey Stent took it.

From the ridge crest, Clay Hanford and Frank Billings watched as the flames began to lick from doorways and windows of the cabins and take their first bite on the outer walls. Though it was the last that had been touched off, the feed shed was the first to be flames from end to end. Hanford stirred restlessly in his saddle.

"I never did a thing like this before," he said soberly. "And I'm not proud of it. Like Pikey Stent said — it's a hell of a note when men begin burning one another out. But some things seem to be thrust upon a man; he uses the weapons at hand or he loses the fight."

"Don't you go to feeling one damn bit bad, Clay," Frank Billings said. "I'm sure not. Once I had a cabin of my own. Maybe Tap told you about it. I built it myself, over on the South Fork of May Day Creek. Fixed it up just the way I wanted it. If there's any truth in the claim that a man's home is his castle, then that cabin was my castle.

"I ran a few head of cattle, just enough to get me by. I didn't yearn to grow big, to throw my weight around. All I wanted was to be left alone, able to come in from a day of work and stand in the doorway of a cabin that was my own. It was damned little I asked of the world, Clay. Even so, they wouldn't let me have it. They burned me out!"

"Morgan?"

"And the rest. LeBard, Siebold — probably Acuff. They ran with Morgan then, just like now. Yeah, they burned me out. So, there are no regrets in me over that fire yonder. I'm ready and willing to light some more!"

In silence they watched the flames climb, break through the cabin roofs. Watched the smoke bloom and pillar against the sky. After which they dropped across the ridge and headed back through the tangle of the hills toward their own camp in the big timber above Lyle Canyon.

Riding the trail he had chosen, Pikey Stent looked back just twice. Each time he went off into a spasm of thin cursing. For now he was without a home and at a loss just where to head. He finally decided on town.

He kept south of Buck Siebold's Long S and took the cutoff trail which ran through the east end of Reservation range. When well along it, he found Cob Jacklyn holding down the middle of it. Jacklyn eyed the tangle of gear tied to Pikey's saddle.

"You must be heading out. Where to?"

"Town. Lookin' for Frenchy, too. You seen him?"

Jacklyn shook his head. "What you want him for? Tell him you're quitting, maybe?"

"Hell — no!" snapped Pikey spitefully. "Tell him he ain't got no more headquarters."

Cob Jacklyn rocked a little forward in his saddle. "I saw a drift of smoke up that way. You mean — ?"

"That's right," Pikey nodded. "Burned to the ground. Frank Billings and that new feller I heard tell of — that Hanford — well, they showed all of a sudden, gave me a couple of minutes to round up some of my gear, then touched off the whole shebang; cabins, feed shed — all of it. And a hell of a note, I say! Damn country's gone crazy. And while he was doin' it, this Hanford made some kinda fool talk about an eye for an eye and a knife that cut two ways at once."

"Quite so — quite so!" murmured Jacklyn, a faint break of sardonic humor showing in his cheeks. "An eye for an eye! One of the oldest laws in the book, Pikey. Written a long time ago. By some very wise men. Nothing they've figured out since has improved on it."

What little intelligence Pikey Stent had been born with had long since become more or less moribund through monotony and lack of mental stimulation of any kind. So, as when Clay Hanford had spoken along the same lines back at the ranch, Pikey wasn't sure just what Cob Jacklyn was driving at.

"I dunno nothin' about them old laws," he blurted. "All I know is it's a hell of a note when a man is burned out."

"Yes," agreed Jacklyn, "it is. But others should have given that possibility a little thought."

Pikey held still as a random thought sifted through the torpid processes of his mind. He fixed Jacklyn with a rheumy stare.

"Sa-ay — didn't I hear you'd quit Crown?"

"Probably. Because I did."

"What for? You had a good spot there."

"Not good enough, Pikey — not good enough. Not enough pay for what I'd had to do to earn it."

Pikey blinked over this. "You were foreman. What more'd you want?"

"Maybe the right to hang on to a little self-respect," Jacklyn said. Then, with a sort of introspective soberness he added, "And there were all the values of what might have been, that Morgan was robbing me of."

Pikey blinked some more, before shrugging. "This self-respect business and them other things you're talkin' about don't make any sense to me. Way I see it, a bellyful of grub, regular, and a dry place to sleep — them's all that counts."

"Plenty to eat and a dry bed keeps a dog happy, too," said Jacklyn drily.

Pikey thought that over for a moment, felt vaguely that there was a barb in it somewhere, but couldn't put his finger on it. He grunted and rode on.

Some two miles further along, the trail Pikey was on came in at the junction of Fandango and May Day Creeks. Here Pikey met up with two more riders. King Morgan and Speck Mastick. Morgan eyed Pikey harshly.

"Where the hell you running to?"

Pikey gulped. He'd always felt cowed and fearful in the presence of King Morgan. For that matter, Pikey Stent stood in fear of a lot of people, his boss, Frenchy LeBard for one. But never with quite the awe this towering, implacable, bitter-faced cattleman inspired. Under the punishing emphasis of Morgan's words he cringed and made fumbling reply.

"I ain't runnin', Mister Morgan. It's only that —"

"If you're not running," broke in Morgan, "where you going with all your gear?"

"Just — headin' for town. Had to go somewhere. Ain't nothin' left at Sixty-six."

"Nothing left at Sixty-six! What are you talking about?"

"The fire."

"Fire?"

"That's it. Everythin' gone — burned."

As Cob Jacklyn had done at this same word, King Morgan came forward in his saddle. "How did it happen?"

"Frank Billings and that feller Hanford, they done it. Run me out, ready to throw down on me with a gun if I argued. Then they touched things off. Last I see of the place it's burnin' like hell awheelin'. That's the truth of it, Mister Morgan."

There was no doubting Pikey's story. Morgan twisted in his saddle with blunt order for Speck Mastick.

"Get down across Reservation. Stay with the creek. You'll find Frenchy and Siebold somewhere along it. Everybody gather at Sixty-six. I'll be there, waiting."

Mastick nodded and swung away. Morgan brought his harsh glance back to Pikey Stent.

"Which way did they come in at Sixty-six, and which way did they leave?"

Pikey blinked, recalling. "I dunno just how they come in. I was inside, and first thing I knew they was right outside the door. But when they left, they cut up the front of the ridge to the west."

Pikey waited for King Morgan to say something more, but now the cattleman seemed to have lost all interest in him, swinging his horse around until he was looking north and west, in the general direction of Sixty-six. He tipped his head back slightly, as though searching for smoke against the sky. But between this spot and Sixty-six headquarters, lay time, distance and the more concrete barriers of timber and upthrown ridges.

Pikey began edging his horse along, a mean little man with all inclination to mix in real trouble long since drained out of him. He fairly held his breath, expecting harsh order to come back. He reached a bend in the trail, got around it and immediately stirred his horse to a faster pace, to a jog, which set his various bundles of gear to jouncing around him.

Pikey Stent was eager for town. He couldn't get there fast enough. And maybe, considering the look he'd just seen on King Morgan's face, he wouldn't even stop in town. Not for too long, anyhow. Maybe, if a man was real smart, he'd get to hell plumb out of Fandango Basin. Because there were shadows settling down all across it. Not the kind of shadows a man could see, but the kind he could feel — the kind that put a weight on his head and a settled chill up his spine.

King Morgan did not immediately head for Sixty-six. It would, he knew, take time for Speck Mastick to locate the others and get the word around. But this was the thing they'd been searching for — a trail that was fresh and definite.

On leaving Crown early this morning, no one had any idea where they might pick up such a trail of Clay Hanford and Frank Billings. For Fandango Basin was big country, and to ride it blindly on the chance of bumping into Hanford and Billings could be an aimless business that would wear out men and horses to no useful end.

There were a thousand places Hanford and Billings might lie temporarily safe hidden against discovery. This King Morgan knew. But he knew also that they could not hide all the tracks their horses must leave. It was like trailing any quarry. You looked for sign, and when you found it you worked it out, patient and relentless. In time that sign must lead you to the quarry. So then you had it in the open in front of you where you could work your will upon it.

And it was this fact that Morgan had in mind when he scattered his men, to search all up and down Fandango Creek and along the trails crossing it.

He was not too surprised at the word Pikey Stent had given him. With his own headquarters burned, Hanford had struck back in kind at Sixty-six. But, mused Morgan, with savage satisfaction, this was Hanford's big mistake. For he had left a strong, fresh trail. And no matter where or how he rode it, it would do him no good; he was bound to leave some sign of his passing. And so, patience, tenacity, grim purpose — these must run him to earth.

Morgan brought his glance back to the trail and touched his horse with the spur, then abruptly reined up again. Riding down the trail toward him was Cob Jacklyn, a high, spare shape in the saddle. Jacklyn's horse took the slight dip of the trail to the creek crossing, splashed through and climbed the near bank to within half a dozen paces of Morgan. Past a level stare, Jacklyn said:

"Well, King."

Morgan's answer was a harsh, unforgiving growl. "You damned traitor!"

Jacklyn's glance did not waver. "You called me that once before. I told you then that before long you and I would have an understanding. That time is now!"

Jacklyn spoke quietly. But there was in his tone and manner, in the slightly narrowed, dead-level glint in his eye, in the all-over look of him, something that was as cold and implacable as Morgan's own purpose. It was a sweep of chill wind, blowing upon a man.

"Yes," Jacklyn went on, "the time is now. Being the sort you are, I doubt you'll understand. Yet I will have my say. King, a man has only so many really good years of life — the years when he gives of his strength and will to climb the mountain, the years before he passes the crest and begins coasting down the other side. Those are the rich years, when a man builds either for himself, or for someone else.

"Well, I built for someone else. I built for you. I gave those good years to Crown. I ran your ranch for you, King — and I made it a good ranch. I was faithful to your every interest. I watched your kids grow up, and having none of my own, I knew a fondness for them. Even when you began the big change, from a stern, but just man, into a power crazy, unjust one, I still stayed faithful, hoping you'd come back to your senses. Instead, you got worse."

"Hell with you!" broke in Morgan savagely. "Hell with that mealy-mouthed talk. You're a damned traitor. Get out of my way!"

He started his horse ahead.

"No!"

Jacklyn swung his horse at right angles across the trail. His right hand slid past his hip, then rested across his saddle horn, and it was filled with the ominous bulk of blue-black gun metal. King Morgan again drew rein.

"Better!" Cob Jacklyn said. "There's more, and you're going to listen to it. Because there's a reason to what's ahead, and I want you to know the all of it. No, you didn't come back to sanity — you got worse. You did your damndest to poison your own kids with your craziness. You did a job of it with Price. He was becoming you, all over again. And now he's dead, killed by that craziness. I figure there's still some hope for Lute, if he can get away from you. While Lear — she's had the meanest deal of all."

Off in the timber a bluejay gave strident call. Jacklyn went still, listening, for a jay's startled call could often announce a presence of some sort. Slow minute ticked by while Jacklyn waited tautly, never taking his eyes off Morgan. Presently he relaxed and went on.

"I said it. Lear had the mean deal. She was a good girl who tried to be a good daughter to you. You wouldn't let her. You were just too busy making yourself big, too busy playing at being God. You never gave that girl even a little of the kind of life she was entitled to. No, she was just another of your possessions. You ran young Tap Timberlake — a good boy — away from her and tried to make her friendly up to that stupid, bull-necked gorilla — Buck Siebold. Why? Because you couldn't handle Tap. But you could handle Siebold and you wanted him on your side. So you dangled Lear in front of him. Why, damn you, Morgan, you came close to using your own daughter like she was some animal to trade for Siebold's good will!"

Outrage built up in Cob Jacklyn's tone, along with the blazing heat of an anger that had been long locked back. And now the first real intimation of what could lie ahead reached King Morgan and settled him still and watchful in his saddle. He spoke mechanically, outside the swift tightening of his thoughts.

"What's mine is mine, and I do with it as I please!"

"Not with Lear," retorted Jacklyn. "She's done with you. She's with Tap, now, nursing him, and there's her happiness. But you would never leave her have it, would you? No, you never would. Because she defied you and Tap defied you, so you'd go after both of them for that. Only, I'm not going to let you go after them. You see, Lear was always my favorite, kind and good to me. And that meant much to me, more than you'd ever understand. So I'm going to see to it that Lear has her chance at happiness. I'm not going to let you ever bother her again. King, you've lived too long!"

Now Morgan had it, had it fully and beyond doubt. He knew now what lay behind that chill remoteness of Cob Jacklyn's first approach and the purpose of his words. This man holding the trail had rendered judgment on him, rendered judgment and pronounced the penalty. This man, Cob Jacklyn, once his foreman and closest confidant, meant to kill him!

It had been long since King Morgan had known actual physical fear, mainly perhaps because it had never entered his mind that any man could successfully stand against him. But here now there was just the two of them — Cob Jacklyn and himself — facing each other in a world that was suddenly still

and poised and vastly lonely. Tension settled coldly in the pit of Morgan's belly. His
voice ran heavy.

"You talk about my sanity. You're the
one who's crazy. What would it serve you to
kill me?"

"It could serve to preserve the ranch I
gave those good years of my life to," Jacklyn
said. "If you continued to live, Crown must
surely be destroyed by other men to keep it
from destroying them. For you'd never
stop, would you, King? Never stop
reaching, grabbing, trying to dominate.
With you gone, Crown has a chance. Lute,
maybe, will take hold and run things fair
and sensible. And Lear will have her share
of it, and her chance for happiness."

Often had King Morgan been implacable
and unyielding with others. Now he was
facing implacability himself. He who had
sat in judgment, was being judged.

He ran the tip of his tongue along his lips.
"We can work this out, Cob. There's not a
single angle we can't work out. Hell, man —
think of the years you and me — !"

"No!" Jacklyn cut in ruthlessly. "That
won't do, won't do no good at all. Did you
think of those good years when you chose
between me and that back-shooting whelp,
Frenchy LeBard? What did those years

273

mean to you then? Nothing — not a damned thing! I had an opinion. It wasn't your opinion. I wouldn't say yes to you, but LeBard would. So you took him over me. King, you never in your life forgave any other man for doing you a hurt, so let's not have you asking for it now!"

If fear had been a common thing with him, perhaps King Morgan might have found some means of hiding it. But he had no such means now and it leaped up stark and ugly in every bitter twist of his face. His lips pulled away from his teeth in a grimace that was wild and wickedly hating.

"King," said Cob Jacklyn, almost gently, "you're making it easier for me all the time!"

King Morgan drove home the spurs, sawing on the reins, bringing his horse up and around in a rearing, lunging spin. He clawed at his gun and threw a hurried, desperate shot and knew he had missed. He tried another, frantically, shooting almost back across his shoulder as his horse whirled. And knew this one missed, too.

Cob Jacklyn was unhurried, icily deliberate. Twice he looked for Morgan over the sights of his leveled weapon, and twice he corrected on a rearing, whirling target before letting off his shot.

Morgan's spur and bit punished horse

came down with plunging hoofs that chopped the earth and spun it completely around. King Morgan was still in the saddle, but now he was queerly hunched. The horse came all the way around again, but when this spin was finished, the animal was under empty saddle. King Morgan lay beside the trail, face down, still and shrunken.

The echoes of report ran out into the timber and died there. Stillness came down on a startled world, with only the gusty breathing of a riderless, restless horse to break it.

Cob Jacklyn's mount, restless too, tossed its head, backed and sidled. Its rider stared down with tired, bitter eyes at the still figure of King Morgan. After which, Cob Jacklyn holstered his gun and reined out along the trail for town.

THIRTEEN

Around mid-afternoon Lute Morgan rode into town and tied at the Ute House rail. He had washed away all removable effects of his fight with Speck Mastick and had donned a clean shirt, and while several bruises marked his face, his eyes were clear and steady and direct. Mike Scorry met him at the door.

"Lear?" asked Lute.

"Inside," nodded Mike, his round face gravely sober. "Glad you're here. Now you can break the news to her, which is the way it should be, what with the two of you being brother and sister and the last of your family."

Lute hauled up, completely still. "Last of the family?"

"Then you haven't heard?" Mike Scorry dropped a hand on Lute's arm. "Lute, your father is gone."

"Gone! You don't mean — ?"

Mike nodded. "That's it. He's dead."

It was something that had to be said and there was no way in which it could be softened. Lute rocked as though from a physical blow. Where he found words they were tight and strained.

"How do you know?"

"I have seen him," Mike said simply. "I went out with Doctor Klaus and Ben Strike to bring him in."

"Bring him in from where?"

"The flat where Fandango and May Day Creeks join. We took one of Ben Strike's wagons from his freight yard."

"How — did it happen?"

"He got in a shoot-out, Lute."

"With that fellow Hanford?" Lute's voice rang savagely.

Mike shook his head. "Not Hanford."

"Then — who?"

"Coming to that," Mike said evenly. "The man who killed your father was the one who told me where to find him. The showdown was between King Morgan and Cob Jacklyn."

"Cob Jacklyn! I can't believe that. It could never be."

"But it was," reasserted Mike. "Right on this very porch Cob Jacklyn stood and looked me in the eye and told me what had happened, and why."

Lute was frozen to stillness again, trying to get the grim import solidly in his mind.

Now the growing up process that had begun last night, reached its full completion. Slowly the strained stiffness drained out of him, while a bleakness settled in his eyes which reflected an intent and purpose beyond all mistaking. His voice ran even and curt.

"I want to see this fellow Jacklyn. Where'll I find him?"

"You won't," Mike said. "He's gone, out of Fandango Basin and these parts for good."

"I'll go after him."

"Which would serve no sensible purpose at all," Mike declared. "Besides, he left word for you."

"What kind of word?"

"He said to tell you that he did what he did, for the sake of Lear and you — and Crown."

Press of emotion set Lute's face to working again. "Of all the damned hypocritical talk — !"

"I wonder," murmured Mike. "Ever since he said it I've been mulling the thing over in my mind, and I feel I know what he meant and how he meant it."

"You're agreeing that Jacklyn did Lear and me a service by — by killing our father?" flared Lute bitterly. "Just what the hell are you trying to say to me, Scorry?"

"I'm saying this," returned Mike quietly. "I'm saying I can understand why you should feel as you do this moment. But also I'm saying that given time, you may feel differently, and perhaps even understand a little of what Jacklyn meant."

"I understand only one thing," Lute said harshly. "Cob Jacklyn killed my father. He admits the fact. For that he answers to me. I'll find him, all right. I'll find him if I have to trail him through hell!"

"And should you do so," Mike retorted, "you'll be Creation's greatest fool. And make Jacklyn's sacrifice all for naught."

"Sacrifice!" cried Lute. "You call what he did a sacrifice on his part?"

"Ay!" Mike growled. "That I do. He had to kill a man he'd ridden for all the good years of his life; a man he'd once considered his best friend. Do you think he found any pleasure in that? You know better. King Morgan lies dead this day because, of his own will and choosing, he rode a trail that was certain to end exactly as it did. If not at the hands of Cob Jacklyn, then certainly at those of someone else.

"Lute, your father was wrong in this thing — wrong all the way. Why was your brother Price killed? Because he rode on a predatory raid. Who planned and ordered and headed that raid? King Morgan, your father did. Why is Lear, your sister, inside my hotel this minute, sitting at the bedside of Tap Timberlake? Why did she stand in this doorway and defy King Morgan and refuse to return home with him? Because he was wrong. Understand — wrong! And had you ridden with him this day, then you wouldn't have had to learn of his death from me. But you didn't ride with him, did you, Lute?"

It was some little time before Lute answered. Then he shook his head and spoke in a low voice.

"No. I stayed at the ranch."

"And why did you?"

Lute moved to the edge of the porch, stood staring at the street. "Because I wouldn't agree with what he had in mind."

"Which was to keep on after Clay Hanford?"

"Yes."

Mike exclaimed softly. "Good lad! Cob Jacklyn's estimate of you was correct. Last night King Morgan and others, they burned out Hanford's headquarters on Reservation. Did you know of that?"

Lute nodded. "I know. I was there. I — didn't like it. How did you learn?"

"Jacklyn told me. Well, this morning, as

might be expected, Hanford hit back in kind. He and Frank Billings caught LeBard away from Sixty-six and burned it to the ground. Pikey Stent came through town with that word.

"Lute, it might have been Crown that Hanford touched off. And if so, who could blame him? That man has every legal right to be in this basin, to take over Reservation. And he never wanted any trouble. He stood right in my barroom the first night he was in town and declared himself for all to hear. He wanted no trouble. But trouble was thrown at him. And who threw it? You know who threw it. Now your father is gone and your brother, Price — he's gone, too. But Crown remains and it is yours, and Lear's. You can make it the ranch it was before, and keep it so — by stopping this trouble, now!"

For some little time Lute stayed as he was, staring at the street. Afternoon sun struck warmly and the timber tops beyond town were etched in stillness against the sky's wide blue. When Lute finally turned he was grave and quiet.

"Where is — father?"

"In the stage station. Doctor Klaus laid him out decently."

Lute glanced toward the stage station,

then moved to the hotel door.

"Lear will have to know, of course. I'll tell her." He paused to look Mike Scorry levelly in the eye. "Thanks for everything, Mike — including straightening out my thinking for me. You're right, of course."

"Room Two, Lute," Mike said.

The door of Room Two was open. Lute stood quietly in it for a moment. Inside, Lear was bending over a weak, but conscious Tap Timberlake, fussing with his pillows. Both she and her patient were smilingly intent on each other.

Lute stepped in and closed the door behind him. In this room there would be some tears. But also in here was youth, and youth had resilience and an ever-eager reaching for the future.

Shortly after early dark, Clay Hanford and Frank Billings rode in at Morgan Junction and left their mounts in the usual deep shadow beyond Gorman's store. They surveyed the starlit street warily, noting the several mounts in front of the Golden, the three in front of the Ute House and the two, plus a buckboard at Gorman's rail.

"Crowded more than usual," Frank Billings observed laconically. "Why for, d'you suppose?"

"King Morgan could be holding another

meeting," suggested Hanford.

"Maybe," Billings agreed. "He's hell on meetings." Then, drily, "I doubt we'd be welcome. Fact is, by the look of things, maybe we better postpone visiting Tap until some time when things are a little less crowded. Else we could end up plumb to our necks in a little pot of hell."

Soberly thoughtful, Hanford did not answer right away.

That morning, after their strike at Sixty-six headquarters, he and Billings had returned to their Lyle Canyon camp in a roundabout manner, deliberately fashioning a trail calculated to confuse. At one point they struck Fandango Creek well to the west, rode down the middle of it for a good half mile, left it on the south bank and swung south east to Piute Creek, following this to within some three miles of Hack Williamson's Running W headquarters, then heading back west and north once more through the aspen brakes above Lyle Canyon, there crossing Fandango Creek once more to come finally into the big timber and their camp.

By the time this was done it was midday, and the following long, still hours of the afternoon had got on Clay Hanford's nerves. Frank Billings made easier going of it. He had an older man's philosophical patience, along with a knack of making little things do, and he had killed the afternoon making some minor repairs on his riding gear.

A time, Hanford had watched at this. Afterward he set himself to gathering firewood. But he soon had enough of this to last for a week. He tried then to sleep some of the time away, but that did not work out very well, either. For his thoughts would not leave him be.

He had a lot at stake in the way of future in this Fandango Basin. Here was the opportunity of his life. Here also, obstacles and risks. Neither of these daunted him. But essentially, he had always been a man of action, and the present situation contained a hit or miss uncertainty that was deeply frustrating.

Always the realist, Hanford knew that few fights were ever won by purely negative action. To win, a man had to move positively; he had to carry the fight and call the moves. The fact that he had reacted in kind to the burning of his headquarters by touching off Sixty-six, was not necessarily positive action. Rather was it reaction to action, a retaliatory blow at a minor opponent.

Crown was the outfit he had to topple to

win this thing, and Crown meant King Morgan. Yet he held no deep down desire to destroy either the ranch or the man. He would fight any man in defence of what was rightfully his, and he might be ruthless to the extent the opposition was ruthless. But like any sensible person he preferred less extreme measures. He still clung to the hope that some way some sort of agreement could be arrived at with Crown, without the need of more gunfire and violence and destruction.

He considered the possibility, now that King Morgan's eldest son lay dead because of such violence, that the cattleman might listen to reason. Perhaps, if some kind of meeting with King Morgan could be arranged through the offices of a substantial, neutral man like Hack Williamson, this thing could be settled without further bloodshed. It might be worth a trial.

So had Clay Hanford's thoughts run as he waited out the afternoon. For this was, he had mused savagely, a hell of a way for a man to have to live. To skulk and hide and lay a tangled trail behind him in hopes it could not be followed. Like a criminal, or some outlaw renegade! The unrest had piled up in him until toward evening he had announced his determination to ride to town and see how Tap Timberlake was coming along, and risk be damned!

So, now they were in town, and from the looks of the street, there could be plenty of risk, and also plenty of basis for Frank Billing's wry summation of the immediate possibilities.

Two men stepped from the door of Gorman's store and Hack Williamson's voice struck strongly across the night. There was wrath in it.

"The hell with LeBard and Siebold and Acuff! If they think, now that King Morgan's dead, they're going to take on where he left off, and run this basin like they owned all of it, they got another think coming. There's been a big plenty of that high and mighty stuff. Sure I'll talk with them, but they're going to be told a few facts of life. From now on, if anybody takes over the leadership of these parts, it'll be me — Hack Williamson. And I'm a man of peace, and I intend to have peace, if I have to kill somebody to get it!"

Hack Williamson and Speck Mastick moved out of the yellow light flow from the store's open door, dropped into the comparative darkness of the street and crossed through this to the Golden.

"Clay, did you hear what I heard?" questioned Frank Billings with quick softness. "King Morgan — dead!"

"I heard," answered Hanford. "And I want to know more about it. Come on!"

They climbed to the porch of the store. As they did so, the tall, lank figure of Joe Gorman came through the door, to stand staring over at the Golden. Startled, he came around swiftly when Hanford spoke.

"Joe, what's this I hear about King Morgan being dead?"

Lamplight, thrusting from the open door, glistened on Gorman's naked head as he nodded.

"It's true enough. He's dead."

"When did it happen, and how?"

"This morning, sometime. Him and Cob Jacklyn got in a shootout."

"Cob Jacklyn!" exclaimed Frank Billings. "What do you know! With him being Crown foreman for so many years. What set them against each other?"

Joe Gorman shrugged. "All I know is that Jacklyn quit Crown two or three days ago. Then they bump into each other out along one of the trails, and whatever their argument is, they settle it, permanent. Jacklyn brought the word, himself. Told Mike Scorry about it and where to find Morgan. Mike and Ben Strike and this doctor who's lookin' after Tap Timberlake, they went out in one of Ben Strike's wagons and brought Morgan in. And sa-ay, accordin' to what Pikey Stent told, here in town, you two fellers been raising a little assorted hell, yourselves. Pikey said you burned Sixty-six. Ain't that pretty rough business?"

"Pretty rough," Hanford agreed. "But LeBard helped burn us out, so we decided to see how he liked some of his own medicine. Where's this fellow Jacklyn, now?"

"He's pulled out. Left the basin."

Hanford tipped his head toward the Golden.

"What's going on over there?"

"Something I ain't too easy about," said the lank storekeeper. "LeBard and Siebold and Acuff, they sent Speck Mastick after Hack Williamson with some kind of message. I didn't get what Mastick said to Hack, but judgin' from Hack's reply, I'd guess that LeBard and Siebold and Acuff — now that King Morgan is dead — are cookin' up some kinda wild ideas which Hack don't intend to stand for. And I don't like the idea of him being in there alone with that crowd, arguing with them. Acuff don't amount to much, not bein' near as tough as he looks. But Siebold and LeBard — especially LeBard — they could be bad medicine. I wouldn't trust either of them from here to you. And I wouldn't trust Speck Mastick, either. I got a notion to get me my counter gun and take a walk over yonder."

"An idea, Joe," Hanford said quickly. "Maybe we'll take that walk with you. Williamson in town alone?"

"His women folks are with him. They're up at the Ute House with Hannah Scorry."

"You go get that gun," Hanford said.

Gorman ducked into the store. Hanford turned to Frank Billings.

"All right with you, Frank?"

"Hell, yes! You heard Hack say the kind of stand he's going to take. Well, that's our stand, too, ain't it?"

"There a back way into the Golden?"

"Yeah."

"Take it. But don't show yourself unless you have to. If you have to, then you'll know what to do."

"I'll know," affirmed Billings briefly. "Give me a couple of minutes." He dropped into the darkness of the street and hurried away.

In the Golden, Hack Williamson stood halfway along the bar and had his good look around. At the far end of the bar, Coony Ells stood, hulking and, heavy, a whiskey glass in one hand, some free lunch in the other, alternating between the two with greedy gulps. Beyond him was Dave Rich of Crown, also working hungrily at Pete Garth's free lunch. At one of the poker tables, Frenchy LeBard, Buck Siebold and Rusty Acuff sat, drinks in front of them. Speck Mastick, after entering with Hack Williamson, circled and took a chair at the same table, forming a pattern that was unmistakable. Behind the bar, Pete Garth stood quietly watchful.

Hack Williamson surveyed the four at the poker table. All of them were rough and unkempt, as if from too much riding and too little sleep. Frenchy LeBard was more venomously wolfish than ever, and Buck Siebold never more the surly, thick-necked brute. Rusty Acuff, with his scarred face, appeared somewhat withdrawn, slouched far down in his chair, his hat low over his eyes. Speck Mastick sat higher in his chair, calculatingly watchful, as if judging which way the light and shadow fell most strongly, so that he might shift accordingly. Hack Williamson's lips curled slightly.

"You wanted to see me," he said brusquely. "Here I am!"

Frenchy LeBard flared a little. "Sounds like you might have a chip on your shoulder, Williamson. If so, get rid of it. The talk coming up is for the good of all of us."

"I'll be the judge of whether it's good for me," shot back Williamson drily. "Let's hear it."

"All right — here it is. King Morgan ain't around any more to lead things. But me and Buck are. And from you, Williamson, we want it, straight up and down, just where you're going to stand. The old neutral talk won't do any more. In the past you been lettin' others pack the load while you got in on the gravy. And that ain't good, the way Buck and me see it. So now, either you play along with us, the way we want things, or we'll figure you're against us. And that won't be good either — for you!"

Williamson eyed LeBard narrowly. "You and Siebold and Acuff are here to speak for yourselves, and I'm here to speak for myself. Who's speaking for Crown?"

"I am," Speck Mastick said.

Williamson's glance touched him. "That's not good enough for me, Mastick. You just ride for Crown. But the ranch belongs to Lute and Lear Morgan, now, and I don't see Lute here to speak for it."

"Lute'll do what I tell him to do," Mastick declared.

The sardonic curl to Hack Williamson's lips grew more pronounced.

"That I doubt, too. In fact, I'm no way sure you're even riding for Crown any more, now that Lute's the boss. For I hear rumors that he whipped the tall hell out of you this morning. Which sounds reasonable to me, because either he or somebody sure branded you in spots."

Dull, angry color swept through Mastick's face, darkening some already staining bruises. His retort was blurting.

"He got the jump on me. Next time I'll show him . . . !"

Williamson's attention was already back on the others.

"No kind of talk means anything until everybody can sit in on it. And I say again, Lute Morgan isn't here."

"I'll take care of Lute — and Crown," Buck Siebold said.

"Well, well — somebody else going to run Crown, eh?" Hack Williamson's tone was caustic. "I don't think so, Siebold. I doubt that from now on anybody is going to take care of Lute and Crown but Lute himself."

"All right — all right!" said Frenchy LeBard harshly. "Let's just forget Lute Morgan and Crown for the minute. Let's get back to you, Hack, and we want to know. Where you aiming to stand from here on out?"

"Where I've always stood and always will," came Williamson's blunt and ready answer. "On my own principles."

"You're kinda friendly with this feller Hanford, ain't you? You loaned him a wagon?"

"I did. And for the best of reasons. What's it to you?"

"Plenty! Hanford burned me out this morning. Burned me plumb to the ground."

"And you helped burn him out last night," Williamson shot back. "What's the matter, LeBard — your own medicine too strong for you?"

LeBard swung up against the table tautly, eyes moiling.

"I guess that places you, Williamson."

"I guess it does." The line of Hack Williamson's jaw hardened. "I'll make it really clear, LeBard. The high and mighty stuff in Fandango Basin is a thing of the past. It died when King Morgan died. I'll fight you or any other man who tries to take up where King Morgan left off. Now you know!"

Frenchy LeBard's glance searched the cattleman carefully.

"When you make that kind of talk, Williamson, you should carry a gun!"

"My not having a gun with me wouldn't hold you back if there weren't so many witnesses," Williamson told him, his words dripping contempt. "But if that's the way you want it, I'll start carrying one. For there never was a day when I was afraid of a standoff with a damned renegade mongrel like you!"

Frenchy LeBard hit his feet, cadaverous face twisted, eyes moiling murderously, right hand dipping downward.

"Go ahead," taunted Williamson. "Play it real safe, LeBard — in your usual way. Wait until my back's turned, even if I haven't got a gun on me!"

"Different here, Hack. I got a gun." While he spoke, Clay Hanford stepped past the swinging door of the Golden. "And here is what I've been waiting for. Hack, get out of the way!"

Startled, Williamson swung back against the bar, and then Hanford was swiftly past him and facing Frenchy LeBard, who hissed his surprise almost soundlessly.

"Yes," Hanford reiterated harshly, "I've been waiting for this. Since the night you shot Reed Challis in the back, LeBard, I've wanted to come up with you. For you murdered him because he made you crawl. Now I'm going to make you crawl. I'm going to take your gun away from you and whip you with a quirt. While you crawl, LeBard —

crawl literally, on your hands and knees. All the length of the street outside. On your hands and knees. Frank!"

"Right here," Frank Billings said, moving up out of the shadows at the rear of the room.

"Watch Siebold — Acuff — the rest."

"I'm watching," said Billings laconically, "and everybody better believe I am!"

Buck Siebold's heavy face showed a mixture of surly anger and indecision. His chair creaked as he stirred his thick bulk. Beside him, Rusty Acuff spoke with a thin weariness.

"Don't be a fool, Buck. I told you it would be this way. So far we've lost every bet, ain't we? Well, that's it. Some men you just can't beat. He's one of them." Acuff looked at Clay Hanford.

Siebold quieted. Speck Mastick made as if to push back his chair and get to his feet, but stopped the move at Frank Billings's curt warning.

"Stay pat, Mastick! It's too late for you to crawl down on the right side of the fence."

These swift moving factors were registering at the outer fringe of Clay Hanford's awareness, giving of their import, but in no way interfering with his bleakly centered intent on Frenchy LeBard. For he knew what had to be done with this man if other and better men were to move in peace and safety through Fandango Basin. Bad as King Morgan's fanatic, arrogant rule had been, it would be far worse if such as LeBard made attempt to take over Morgan's saddle. And from what he had heard, while listening at the door of the Golden, Hanford now knew that such was LeBard's intent.

Burly brute as he was, Buck Siebold was basically a follower, not a leader. Lacking a leader, Siebold could be kept in line. The same was true of Rusty Acuff, another follower. But LeBard was prowling, predatory — the sort to aspire to leadership, who would plan and scheme and strike treacherously. While he lived, Frenchy LeBard was dangerous as a coiled rattlesnake.

A high alertness held Clay Hanford. It was like a taut, brightly singing wire that was in contact with every nerve end in his body. In a rugged, fundamental past it had been like this a time or two before. When the issue was basic, starkly grim, and when there could be no withdrawing or weakening of purpose. His words struck at LeBard again.

"Get rid of your gun!" he ordered. "Unbuckle your belt and let it drop. Then you get your whipping. With a quirt. While you crawl on your hands and knees, up and down the street where all can watch. You hear me, move — damn you, move!"

Frenchy LeBard moved. Not to take off his gun, but to reach for it, which was what Clay Hanford had planned on from the first. In consequence he was set for the first flicker of movement and acted on it. He drew and fired and was there first.

The impact of Hanford's bullet lifted Frenchy on his toes and folded his shoulders forward. For a breath he hung that way, gun drawn but angled ahead and down. Dying fingers got off a shot that drove splinteringly through the table top. After which LeBard fell forward across the table, rolled clear of it and to the floor, where his booted feet drummed a time or two, then went eternally still.

A vacuum of silence followed the thudding rumble of the shots, broken presently by the even advice of Frank Billings.

"Rest of you, don't get no ideas! Just let matters stop, right where they are."

Buck Siebold cleared his throat thickly, while staring at Hanford.

"You done that a-purpose," he accused. "You rawhided Frenchy into it a-purpose."

"Yes," admitted Hanford harshly, "I did.

It was something that had to be done."

"Quite so," murmured Hack Williamson. "Something that had to be done."

FOURTEEN

It was two days later. Tap Timberlake was sitting up, propped against a mountain of pillows. His boyish face was thin, but there was a touch of color in his cheeks and his eyes were clear and bright. Clay Hanford surveyed him approvingly.

"Feeling real chipper, eh?"

Tap grinned. "Reckon I'll live. Be a couple of days before I can crawl a saddle again."

"Days — hell!" Hanford exploded sternly. "Weeks, you mean. You're staying right in this bed until Hannah Scorry says different. And she had her orders from Doc Klaus."

"I know. Doc did say I had to stick close to bed for a while, but not just this one."

"What's wrong with this one?" Hanford demanded.

"Not a thing. It's a darn good bed. But there's another out at Crown, and Lute Morgan's going to haul me out to it before too long. I can get well there, same as here."

"So that's it! Going completely over to the enemy."

Tap sobered. "No enemy there, Clay. Not any more."

"I know," Hanford said quickly. "I was just joshing. I saw Hack Williamson and he said he'd had a long talk with Lute. All Lute wants is a fresh start. No grudges, no feuds — just a square, decent shake all around. Took a pretty rough ride to get Lute squared away on the right trail, but he's on it now. Hack told me something else. That you and Lute were going to partner it?"

Tap nodded. "Our ranges border. We figured we might as well combine and make it all one big spread."

"Of course," drawled Hanford, "Lear didn't have anything to do with it?"

Tap flushed and his grin came back. "She had plenty to say. Fact is, it was her idea."

"Which just goes to prove you're a lucky pup," declared Hanford.

"I know," Tap said, simply and quietly. He was silent for a moment, savoring the realization. Then he asked, "Where's Frank!"

"Starting another cabin on South Fork. I'm going to help him with it, and after that he'll give me a hand at a new headquarters at Reservation. Mighty good man, that fellow."

Tap nodded. "Wish I could have been more help to you than I was, Clay."

"Near got yourself killed in my interest, didn't you? What more could you do?"

"I could have been in on that final showdown in the Golden."

Hanford's mood turned somber. "Best figure you're lucky you weren't. No man's ever the better for watching another go out like Frenchy LeBard did."

"He had it coming," Tap insisted.

"Let's say he did. Just the same —" Hanford shrugged and turned toward the door, pausing to roll a cigarette, his face shadowed with brooding. "A man pays a big price for security bought that way."

There was a light step in the hallway and then it was Moira Williamson who came in. She looked at Hanford.

"Hope you don't mind me intruding. But I saw that roan horse of yours at the rail and thought you might be in here." She turned to smile at Tap. "You amaze me, Tap — getting well so fast. Could it be, I wonder, because of a certain special nurse you've had?"

Tap faced up to the gently teasing question manfully.

"Shouldn't wonder, Miss Moira. And she's due back from Crown any time to feed me my supper."

"In which case," said Moira briskly, "visitors better clear out." She turned to Hanford again. "Speaking of supper, Aunt Molly said if I should run across you, I was to bring you out to eat with us. So I have. And you will?"

"Sounds like an order," Hanford agreed.

They rode out of town through an afternoon that was well along. The sun was at a long and ever increasing slant, with the shadows beginning to spread like cool, blue smoke. And there was a silence which Moira finally broke.

"I'm wondering if you enjoy the prospects of the evening. Or is it that you resent my possessive ways?"

He came around in his saddle. "Possessive?"

"Exactly. Possessive. And you may as well get used to them, poor man. For the fates decided it all when you hauled me out of Piute Creek. Now you are stuck with me." There was a gentle smiling in her.

He watched her gravely, while the line of his face softened. He spoke slowly.

"If the fates be responsible for my finding you, then they have been mighty good to me. Do you mind if I say you are very wise, and very lovely — and very dear to me?"

The employees of Thorndike Press hope you have enjoyed this Large Print book. All our Thorndike and Wheeler Large Print titles are designed for easy reading, and all our books are made to last. Other Thorndike Press Large Print books are available at your library, through selected bookstores, or directly from us.

For information about titles, please call:

(800) 223-1244

or visit our Web site at:

www.gale.com/thorndike
www.gale.com/wheeler

To share your comments, please write:

Publisher
Thorndike Press
295 Kennedy Memorial Drive
Waterville, ME   04901